THE PERFECT BODY

FRANKIE BOW

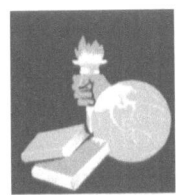

The Perfect Body

Copyright © 2018 by Frankie Bow

Published by Hawaiian Heritage Press

Edited by Carina de Pillis-Shintaku

Chapter One

"ARE YOU OKAY, MOLLY?"

Donnie squeezed my hand a little tighter as we made our way up the worn steps of the old Mahina Memorial Hospital. My normally-stoic husband seemed nervous about our first time leaving the baby alone with the sitter. But instead of coming out and saying so, he kept asking me how I was feeling.

"Donnie, it's fine. Remember I've known Margaret since she was a student. She's probably the most conscientious person I've ever met. And besides, she's already watched Francesca lots of times."

"During the day. With you there."

"That's how I know how good she is with the baby. She's probably reading to Francesca right now from her CPA study guide. Come on, this is our first dinner out together since the baby was born. Let's enjoy it. It's kind of exciting to be out at night, isn't it? Well it is when you've been stuck in the house for two months."

I don't normally look forward to work functions, but the Mahina State University Donor Dinner was different from the team-building retreats our administration regularly inflicted on us. The purpose of tonight's event was to woo and celebrate our donors. There would be no "inspiring" PowerPoint presentations about doing more with less, no mind-numbing exegeses about the distinction between Mission Statements and Vision Statements, no lectures from the Student Retention Office about crafting a "customer-friendly" classroom.

All I had to do tonight was dress up and enjoy a rare dinner out with my handsome husband.

We followed the crowd through the

double doorway into the reception area of the old hospital. The building was in mid-remodel. Here and there you could see a patch of unfinished wood, or wires protruding from the wall where a light switch would be. The tang of fresh drywall cut through the food smells wafting from the dining room.

The old Mahina Memorial Hospital had stood empty for years, accumulating graffiti, termite damage, and ghost stories. Last year, the county had "generously" donated it to the university. It was our white elephant now. But as white elephants went, it was gorgeous.

Donnie and I followed the crowd under one of the two curving staircases that bookended the vast entryway.

"I've always wanted to see what was inside this building," I said. "Look at this. It's like something out of an old movie set."

"It doesn't look ADA-compliant," Donnie remarked. "How do people get upstairs? Is there an elevator?"

That's the kind of thing Donnie would notice. When I enter an old building like this I see glamor and history and long-forgotten craftsmanship. He sees code violations. I would never say it to Donnie, but I think being an entrepreneur eats away a little piece of your soul.

"There's a creaky old elevator somewhere," I said. "You know, the kind I wouldn't ride on a bet. That probably gets us a pass on ADA. Oh! Did you know, Dan, my dean told me he would try to get some space over here for our college? Wouldn't that be amazing?"

"Molly," Donnie said, "*you're* amazing."

He placed his arm around my shoulders as we took our place at the end of what I assumed was the check-in line. I couldn't see the reception table, but from the speed of the line, I assumed there was only one person staffing it.

"You don't like this place," I said.

"It's distinctive," he replied diplomatically. "No offense, but it reminds me a little bit of a horror movie."

"Oh yeah, I can see it. Out of the corner of their eye, someone notices the wallpaper moving. Did they really see a tormented soul screaming? No, it's just the wisteria print. *Or is it?*"

"I thought you didn't like scary movies," Donnie lifted his chin to get a better view of the dining room as we inched forward in line. "This is a distinguished crowd. I see our mayor, two state senators, and a football coach. And there's the prosecutor. Did you know the prosecutor's office used to be in this building?"

"That must have been before I moved to Mahina. This building has been abandoned as long as I can remember."

"You're right. I think the last time anyone was in here was right after I graduated high—graduated *from* high school."

Being much shorter than Donnie, I didn't have the same view he did. But I did get a glimpse of the vast dining room. White-shirted wait staff circulated from one table to the next, refilling water and wine glasses.

"Nice event," he said.

"Don't be too impressed. I wasn't the one who was invited, originally. It was supposed to be Dan, my dean. But he's stuck at an accreditation conference, so he asked me if I wanted to come in his place. Ooh, look at that stamped tin ceiling. Do you think it's original?"

"I suppose so."

I noticed someone waving from a table inside the dining room. I waved back.

"That's Betty Jackson from the psychology department," I said. "She's the one who helped me with the Student Retention Office paperwork. She had a copy of the memo that said we only had to update the Teaching Philosophy Statements once a semester, not every week. It's only the Customer Interaction Reports that every faculty member has to generate each week—"

"Molly?" Donnie interrupted. "We're up. You need to sign in."

"Professor Barda?" I recognized the woman at the registration table as someone who worked in fundraising. Her name tag was hidden behind her hair. "You're at Table Four. Near the entrance, just like you requested. You'll be seated with Miss Dorothy Pfaff and her companion."

"Oh, that'll be nice," I said. "I've met Miss Pfaff. She's delightful."

I hoped it didn't sound like I was namedropping, but it didn't matter in any case. The woman had already turned her attention to Donnie. I was now invisible.

"Congratulations, ah? Donnie. The baby." Apparently, she thought Donnie had managed to produce a baby all by himself. "Aw, I bet she's beautiful. Get pictures?"

Two things about Donnie. One, he's extremely easy on the eyes. Two, he doesn't seem to realize when people are flirting with him.

I do, though.

"Let's not hold up the line." I slid my arm through Donnie's, smiled at the woman, and moved us toward the dining room.

Chapter Two

TABLE FOUR WAS, as promised, close to the entrance. In case of a baby emergency, we could make a quick getaway without disrupting the dinner.

When I saw who was already sitting at Table Four, I wanted to make that getaway immediately.

"Isn't that your old friend, the music teacher?" Donnie asked. "What's his name again? I don't remember."

"Stephen Park. He teaches theater, not music, and he is not my friend."

I wish *I* could forget Stephen Park's name. When I first moved to Mahina,

Stephen and I were briefly an item. We broke up after he stood me up on my birthday. Infuriatingly, whenever I've run into him since then (impossible to avoid on our small campus), he's always acted like he's the wronged party.

"And that's Bee Corcoran sitting with him. She's the new kinesiology professor I was telling you about."

"The one who keeps telling you to work out more?"

"Yes. Nothing a new mom loves better than unsolicited life advice from someone who's never had kids."

"She doesn't look like a man."

"She's not a man. She identifies as a woman. She is a woman. You shouldn't treat her differently or anything. And I'm not sure she wants people to know, so don't tell anyone."

"Then why did you tell me?"

"You're my husband. We're one flesh, remember our wedding vows?"

"Is that the rule?"

"Yes. You tell me everything, right?"

"Sure."

"Come on. It'll be fine. When Dorothy Pfaff shows up she'll talk about her latest skydiving adventure or her affair with Ernest Hemingway or something and we won't have to say a word."

Chapter Three

I DIDN'T DISLIKE Bee Corcoran, exactly. I just didn't want to sit with her. Bee seemed to think I wanted to hear her views on how much to exercise (excessively), what to eat (practically nothing), and how to sleep (for eight uninterrupted hours, "no excuses." Because a baby who wakes up hungry every hour is apparently an "excuse.") I'd never say it to Bee, of course, but I kind of resented getting fitness advice from someone who grew up without thigh fat.

"Molly!" Bee grinned, exposing blue-white teeth. When she reached across the table to grasp my hands, I saw her arm muscles slithering under her skin. She put

FRANKIE BOW

me in mind of a toothy blonde shark sizing up a plump seal.

"Bee, this is my husband Donnie. Of Donnie's Drive-Inn. Donnie, this is Bee Corcoran, our new kinesiology professor."

"Donnie. Hel-*lo*." She turned her high-wattage smile on him and reached out to take his hand.

"Stephen Park, Donnie," I interrupted, "I believe you've met."

This forced the two men to acknowledge each other.

It was only after we were all seated that I noticed Stephen looked different. His black dress shirt was snug over his shoulders, and his neck was thicker (either that or he'd shortened his bolo tie). He looked like he'd been lifting weights, something I'd never known him to do before.

Aside from the new muscles, he was the same old Stephen Park. His jet-black hair was pulled back in a ponytail, as always. Defying the usual order of things, his hairline had advanced, rather than receded. Stephen's parents owned Park Beverly Hills Aesthetic Center. Each time he flew to

12

Southern California to visit them, he came back looking a little younger.

But I noticed glints of silver at Stephen's roots. The eternally-youthful Stephen Park was finally going gray.

It had been a long time, I realized. Years. Maybe it was time to let old resentments go.

"We're very lucky tonight, Bee," Stephen started in as he reached for the bread basket. "We get to sit with the world's happiest couple. Isn't it marvelous?"

Apparently not everyone was letting things go.

Stephen liked to poke fun at my "bourgeois conformity." I had moved on and gotten married, he hadn't, and this was his way of getting back at me. Well, I wasn't going to take the bait. The only thing to do was to maintain a dignified silence.

"Wow, Stephen," I said, "it looks like you lost all of that weight you gained after rehab. Between that and the gray hair, I almost didn't recognize you."

"Oh, he's just eating clean and moving around a little more," Bee said, before Stephen could respond. "Getting in shape's not super hard. You just have to make it a priority. Now, Molly, how about you? Are you taking those walks with the baby?"

"Yes, I am. It's quite invigorating," I said, referring to the times I walked Francesca between the playpen in the living room and the changing table in the nursery. Moving around the house was still moving. "And Francesca loves being carried."

"Be careful about carrying her too much," Bee warned. "You don't want her to get lazy."

"She's two months old, Bee. She's not even going to start crawling for another—"

"Oh, I bet she's *adorable*."

"Well of course she's adorable." Stephen managed a thin smile. "Look at her parents. The ideal family. All they need is one-point-seven more kids and a white picket fence, and the dream is complete."

"The cliché is two point *five* kids, Stephen, not two point seven. So, Bee, how do you like the new building? This is the first time I've been inside. It's so beautiful. They don't build places like this anymore."

"Our Bee is fearless," Stephen

proclaimed. "Aren't you, darling? The ghost stories don't rattle you at all, do they?"

"Hey, I'm just glad to get the lab space I need, finally," Bee said. "I didn't realize how hard it was going to be getting this place up to compliance. We're getting there, though."

"They say if you come here after dark, you can hear babies crying," Stephen said.

"Oh, Stephen, stop trying to scare me!" She dealt him a playful slap on the shoulder, which sounded hard enough to hurt. Stephen didn't seem to mind. "Let's talk about something happy. Do you two have any baby pictures?"

Donnie got there first. He pulled out his smartphone to show off a picture of Francesca in her pink, blue, and white striped knit hospital cap.

"This is Francesca the day she was born." He swiped to the next picture. "And here she is the day we brought her home."

"Oh, she's so cute!" Bee enthused. "Look at all the black hair! She got it from her dad, didn't she? Donnie, you're Hawaiian, aren't you?"

"Hawaiian, Portuguese, Chinese, Scottish, and German," Donnie said.

"I knew it. Lucky girl, there's so much college money out there for Native Hawaiians. You know some of the scholarships I see my Hawaiian students coming in with, wow. I mean I wish I'd had—"

"It's a little early to think about college," I said quickly. Donnie's own college plans had been scuttled in high school when his parents died. "We're just happy to have her. We think she's adorable."

"Yes, *adorable*," Stephen sneered. I wanted to kick him in the shins, but was distracted by a dangerous prickling in my chest. Seeing Francesca's face on Donnie's phone had triggered the letdown reflex. I grabbed my purse and stood up so fast I almost knocked my chair over.

"I have to call the babysitter," I announced, and hurried away, leaving poor Donnie to make conversation with my toxic ex-boyfriend and his tactless companion.

Chapter Four

I RACED INTO A BATHROOM STALL, whipped off my blouse, and checked my pads. I was just in time. Another minute or two and they would have been soaked through. What reckless impulse had led me to wear a red silk blouse? I grabbed a wad of toilet paper and pressed as much moisture out of the pads as I could. In my rush to get out of the house and arrive at the dinner on time, I hadn't even thought about packing an extra pair of breast pads.

Emma Nakamura, my best friend at Mahina State, had advised me not to come to this dinner at all. As I repositioned my bra and bent over to shake everything back into place, I wondered whether she might have been right.

"It's summer," Emma had warned me. "Don't be a schnook and work for free when you should be catching up on your research. It sets a dangerous precedent." (Emma grew up in Hawaii, but went to graduate school in New York. This, in her mind, entitles her to throw in a little Yiddish when she feels like it.)

The flaw in her logic was that doing research is work too. But Emma doesn't see it that way. She lives for her research, which has something to do with plant DNA.

Also, Emma and Yoshi don't have kids, so she has no idea how hard it is to get anything done with a baby in the house. Looking after a baby is like trench warfare —long stretches of boredom punctuated by moments of terror. And like trench warfare, it wears you down. A dinner out, even a work-related one, was a treat.

The donor dinner *should* be a treat, I reminded myself. And I wasn't going to let Stephen Park ruin it.

I tugged my blouse straight, checked the soles of my shoes for stray toilet paper, and headed back out, determined to enjoy my dinner.

Chapter Five

WHEN I GOT BACK to the table, I saw we'd been joined by Geoffrey Gunderson, Mahina State's new Arts and Sciences dean. He was thin, balding, and sixtyish. Emma liked to complain about him, referring to him as "that dithering medievalist with his glasses on his forehead." As far as I could tell, he wore his glasses the usual way. I think Emma only said those things because she resented answering to someone from the humanities.

"Dr. Gunderson," I said.

"Please call me Geoffrey." He stood, beaming, and shook my hand vigorously. "Geoffrey, as in Geoffrey Chaucer, and spelled the same way. Well, of course *you* get the reference, Molly. Molly's secretly one of us, you know. One of these days we might talk her into coming back over from the dark side."

"The dark side?" Bee asked.

"The business school," I explained, as I took my seat. "My Ph.D. was actually in literature and creative writing."

"I bet there's an interesting story there," Bee exclaimed.

"No. Not really."

I had earned my doctorate from a top-ranked program, fully expecting to land a job at an exclusive campus in a trendy city. But the openings simply weren't there. My graduation was followed by a desperate year of gradually broadening my horizons (or "lowering my standards" if you prefer) until I finally landed a position teaching business communication at Mahina State University.

Upon which my dissertation advisor (who has tenure, a pension, and health insurance) wrote to tell me how disappointed he was in me.

"The thing about going over to the dark side," Stephen drawled, "is it pays so well. And who really needs a soul these days?"

"Well," Geoffrey Gunderson rubbed his hands and beamed at us. "What a marvelous concentration of talent we have at this table."

"Geoffrey was sharing some good news about your campus," Donnie said.

"I didn't even ask to be nominated for the system research award." Bee flashed her Sports Illustrated swimsuit smile at her dean. "I'm as surprised as anyone. Honestly."

Stephen reached over and rubbed Bee's back. But he wasn't looking at her. His eyes were on me.

"She's amazing, isn't she?" he said.

A real academic, he may as well have added. *Not some phony who couldn't get a literature position and had to settle for teaching business majors how to pad their resumes.*

I ignored him and turned to Donnie. But Donnie was glaring at Stephen. A little muscle in Donnie's jaw was twitching.

"Well, I didn't only stop by to crow about our accomplishments." Gunderson was rubbing his hands so vigorously now, I half-expected to hear cricket noises. "As impressive as those may be, it's my sad duty to inform you that Miss Dorothy Pfaff won't be joining us tonight after all."

"Oh, what a shame," I said, with genuine disappointment.

"Is Miss Pfaff not feeling well?" Donnie asked.

"No, no, nothing of the kind," Gunderson assured us. "Miss Pfaff is in fine fettle. She's on her way to Buenos Aires right now for a, I believe it's a tango competition of some sort. Her assistant got the dates mixed up. In any event, I wanted to let you know what was happening. But please, stay and enjoy your dinner."

He looked around and lowered his voice. "Please do stay. We need to keep empty seats to a minimum."

"Ah," Stephen said. "Like the Academy Awards."

"Precisely. Precisely," Gunderson said, and then scuttled away, no doubt relieved to escape our dysfunctional table. Donnie reached over and gave my hand a sympathetic squeeze. With Dorothy Pfaff on her way to Argentina, we were staring down the barrel of a long evening with Stephen and Bee.

For a moment I considered faking going into labor. But I'd just had a baby two months ago, so that particular ploy would probably fool very few people.

And then my phone rang.

Chapter Six

"IT'S MARGARET," I said to Donnie.

"I can take it." Before I realized what was going on, Donnie plucked the phone from my hand and was gone.

I couldn't really blame him.

"That was the babysitter calling," I explained.

"Molly, you're so lucky," Bee said. "Donnie seems like such an involved father."

And I'm a very involved mother, although I don't suppose it would occur to anyone to praise me for it.

"He is," I said. "He's wonderful. You're right. I do feel very lucky."

"Indeed," Stephen put in. "I mean, look who you *could've* ended up with."

"I know, right? Bullet dodged." I took a sip of water and didn't look at either Bee or Stephen. What was taking Donnie so long?

Fortunately, a server rolled up to our table with a silver drink cart. She opened her mouth to say something, made brief eye contact with Stephen, and then looked away quickly.

She was tall, slim, and young, with bronze coloring and startling green eyes. Surprisingly, Stephen didn't try to flirt with her.

"Nothing for me," Stephen said flatly, his eyes fixed on the tablecloth in front of him.

Maybe he was afraid Bee would snap him in half if she caught him gawking.

"We'd like green tea," Bee instructed the server.

"Sure thing." The young woman set a box of tea bags on the table. She looked familiar, but I couldn't place her. She wasn't one of my former students. And was it my imagination, or was she looking everywhere except at Stephen?

"What kinds of wine do you have?" I asked.

"Chardonnay, Merlot, and Pinot Noir."

"I'll have Pinot Noir, please."

"They have tea, Molly," Bee said.

I pretended not to hear her.

"Wait," I called to the server as she turned to go. "*They'll* want some too."

"Pinot Noir for them as well?"

"Sure. Yes. Thank you."

I watched the server fill Donnie's glass, and then the glasses at the two empty place settings.

"Impressive, Molly," Stephen said, when the young woman had gone.

"I think the word you're looking for is *thoughtful*, Stephen." I picked up my glass and took a sip. "How would Donnie feel if he came back to an empty wine glass?"

"You know, Molly," Bee said, "if you're concerned about milk production, wine doesn't really help. The thing about wine and beer is a myth. All you need to do is drink plenty of water. The milk glands—"

Stephen pushed his chair back. "It's stuffy in here. I'm going out for a smoke."

"Stephen…" Bee began. But Stephen was already gone.

Now only Bee and I remained, staring at each other across the round table. This was not what I had in mind when I'd talked Donnie into attending the donor dinner with me.

"Love how Mr. Edgy Avant-Garde has to run for the smelling salts the minute someone brings up breastfeeding."

"What was that?" Bee asked.

"What? Oh, nothing, I was just thinking out loud. Apparently. Um, Bee, I notice Stephen's really gotten into shape. Have you been coaching him?"

"Not much. A few tips here and there. But he's very self-motivated. Oh, thank you."

The server had returned with a pot of hot water for the tea.

"One thing, though, he really has to stop smoking," she continued when the young woman had left. She opened the teapot, lowered in three teabags, and closed it again. "I know it's hard to quit, but smoking's about the worst thing you can do for your health. Besides being inactive."

"But they're not *real* cigarettes, Bee." I mimicked Stephen's why-is-everyone-so-stupid inflection. "They're *clove* cigarettes."

"Those are just as bad," Bee said earnestly.

"No, I know about clove cigarettes, I was just..."

Fortunately, Donnie reappeared.

"What did Margaret say?" I asked him. "Is everything okay?"

"Francesca is asleep, but there's only one bottle of breast milk left, and Margaret wanted to know, what if the baby wakes up and drinks the rest of it? I told her go ahead and use the formula. Didn't we go over all that with her before we left?"

"We did." I took back my phone. "But you know Margaret. She has to double-check everything. This is why she's going to be a great CPA."

"Good for you, Molly, sticking with the breastfeeding," Bee said. "You know, you're going to start losing weight eventually if you keep at it."

Once again, I felt an ominous prickling in my chest.

"I'm sorry." I stood up and pushed my chair back under the table. "Will you excuse me for a second?"

"Is it something I can take care of?" Donnie asked, a little too eagerly. I sympathized, but there was nothing to be done.

"No. It is not. I'll just be a second."

Talking about Francesca's feeding had re-activated the letdown reflex. I scurried away, holding my arms up in front of me praying mantis-style.

This time I was too late. As I burst into the ladies' room I saw my reflection. Two maroon splotches bloomed on my red silk blouse.

I cleaned up as well as I could and then poked my head out of the ladies' room to make sure the coast was clear. It was not. Geoffrey Gunderson stood in the entryway between the hallway and the dining room, chatting with someone I couldn't see.

I couldn't walk past Gunderson.

Attempting to scrub the milk off my blouse had only made the stains bigger. And I'd had to throw away my soaking-wet breast pads. To replace them I'd used folded paper towels, which gave me a sort of Cubist silhouette.

Instead of turning left toward the dining room, I turned right to continue down the hallway toward the EXIT sign. The door opened directly to the moonless night outside.

Good. A walk around the building would give my blouse a chance to dry off.

I stepped out onto the rickety landing and let my eyes adjust. It was still warm outside, and a little drizzly. We had walked in on the ground floor, so I was surprised to see several flights of wooden stairs between me and the ground. The dining room was level with the front entrance, but because of the slope of the lot, I was twenty or thirty feet up.

I wasn't sure the stairs would hold my weight. And with no lights and no visible moon or stars, it was completely dark. Fine. I'd go back the way I came, praying-mantis arms and all, and hope no one noticed my stained blouse.

I pulled on the door handle to go back inside. But the door had locked behind me.

Okay, no problem. I'd stick with Plan A. Walk down and around the building and go back through the front entrance. I picked my way down the creaking steps and, happily, made it to the bottom without incident. I switched on my phone light and followed the dirt path, watching the ground for potholes and rocks. The last thing I needed was to trip in the dark and break something.

I caught a whiff of Indonesian clove smoke, and I looked up to see the glow of the end of a cigarette about twenty feet above me. It had to be Stephen up there on the terrace, smoking his stupid cigarettes. I kept my eyes on the ground and kept walking.

"Molly!" I heard Stephen call out above me. I sped up my pace.

"Oh, drop dead, Stephen," I muttered. Whatever he was going to say to me, I didn't want to hear it.

And then I heard something I'd remember for a long time.

Floomp. A heavy sack-hitting-the-pavement kind of sound.

I looked up at the balcony again and strained to see the glow of the cigarette. It wasn't there.

I turned around and shone the light behind me.

What I saw nearly made me drop my phone.

Chapter Seven

I KNOW I DIALED 9-1-1. But only because it's in my call history. I have no memory of making the call.

I remember sirens, and then pulsing blue and red lights in the darkness.

I remember Donnie (how did he get out here?) asking me over and over whether I was okay. I don't remember what I said to him.

I remember Bee Corcoran rushing over to the covered gurney as it was being loaded into the back of the ambulance, and Detective Ka'imi Medeiros stepping in front of her, coming between her and Stephen.

I remember thinking, *no one is supposed to touch the body. Bee should know that.*

At some point Donnie must have taken me home. Although I don't remember that either.

The next thing I recall was waking up in my own bed, to the sound of a ringing phone. I was wearing sweatpants and a worn-out t-shirt.

Donnie was standing in the bedroom doorway, the baby over one shoulder, holding the handset of our phone.

"You're looking for Molly?" Donnie announced loudly. "Just a second, Dan. Let me see if she's here."

I shook my head. No, I was not in any condition to talk to my dean.

"Sorry about that, Dan." Donnie came over to the bed and let me take the baby from him. "She's not available. Can I have her get back to you?"

"Your dad is awesome," I whispered to Francesca as Donnie went off in search of a scrap of paper and a pen.

Chapter Eight

THE BABY OPENED her mouth wide, giving me a glimpse of the sharp tooth breaking through her lower gum. She waggled her head back and forth to find the optimal position and clamped on. Immediately her panic melted away, and her eyelids fluttered and drifted closed. She was motionless except for the plump cheeks, which pulsed gently as she applied an eye-popping level of suction.

I wasn't exactly comfortable, but the baby was happy, which was something.

"Look at you two," Donnie smiled as he came in. "You look so serene."

"I guess," I said. "If 'serene' is a synonym

for the sensation of someone clamping a sawtooth binder clip on your nipple. She's having fun, anyway."

Francesca bit down harder and kicked her chubby legs with delight.

"A sawtooth binder clip? What's that?" Donnie sat on the chair next to the bed.

"I don't know. What did Dan want? Was it about what happened last night?"

"No, it was something about moving your office. I don't know if he knows about last night. He didn't say anything about you-know-what."

"It's fine," I said. "We can discuss it in front of the baby. She's not paying attention. She's busy doing her food-processor imitation."

Donnie stroked my hair. "How are you feeling? It must have been hard for you. Having to see what you saw."

"Uh, yeah."

Here is the horrible truth: I felt more relief than grief at Stephen's death. I was not about to tell Donnie, of course. He'd think I was a heartless monster.

But it was freeing to realize I could show

up at the next department chairs' meeting without having to endure an hour of Stephen's passive-aggressive barbs.

"It's kind of jarring to have someone die right in front of you," I said.

Donnie leaned forward and laid his hand on mine.

"You saw it happen?"

"Well, okay. He didn't literally die in front of me. He died *behind* me if you want to be precise about it."

"Molly, what were you doing back there? I'm not saying it was your fault or anything, I'm just curious."

"You really want to know? Fine. I was trying to avoid running into Geoffrey Gunderson. He was standing right where the hallway opens into the dining room."

"So, you went out the back door instead?"

"Yes. And then the door closed behind me and I was locked out, so I couldn't go back inside."

"But why? I know you don't like talking to people, but you were doing fine. I thought you were very charming."

"The front of my blouse had two big milk stains on it. Plus I was covered with those little paper shreds you get when you try to dry your shirt with a paper towel. Donnie, would you mind...?"

"Sure."

Donnie got up and came back with a pillow and a tall glass of ice water. I positioned the pillow under the baby to ease the strain on my back and downed half the glass in one go.

"Thanks," I said. "Much better."

Donnie sat back down and looked at me with a concerned expression.

"Molly, I—"

"Donnie, you don't have to take the day off. Go take care of the Drive-Inn. Margaret will be here soon."

"That's not what I was going to say."

"You weren't offering to stay home with me?"

"I will if you want me to."

"No, it's fine. What were you going to say?"

"I just wanted to say I know you're

naturally a curious, inquisitive person, and I love that about you."

"But?"

"When you set your mind on something, there's no stopping you. But now we have Francesca, it's not just the two of us. We have to think about—"

"Donnie, can you get to the point? Sorry, that sounded kind of snappish."

"Kind of," he agreed.

"Look, I have an angry little customer here chewing up my tender bits. *Ow*, baby, hang on. Next course is coming right up."

When I had switched Francesca to the other side, I turned my full attention to Donnie.

"Yes? What would you like to tell me?"

"I'm worried you're going to get curious about what happened to Stephen Park, and you're going to get mixed up in something dangerous," he said. "I'm asking you right now. Please don't."

"You're asking me not to look into Stephen's death?"

Donnie nodded.

"Okay."

"Really?"

"Yes, really. Please don't worry. I have no desire to get involved with this. Besides, I didn't even..."

I stopped myself before I could say, *I didn't even want to have anything to do with Stephen Park when he was alive.* It would have come off as callous, I think.

Donnie reached over and squeezed my hand.

"Thank you. Molly, I don't like coming off like I'm telling you what to do. But if it's a choice between that and some crazy murderer pushing you into a lava tube—"

"I guess I'm never living *that* down..." Francesca grunted and jerked her head back and forth. "*Ow!* Come on baby, let's latch you on properly. Geez, what kind of baby starts growing teeth at two months?"

I repositioned Francesca as Donnie averted his eyes.

"It's okay," I said, "You're allowed to look."

"I know. I just don't want to get shot in the eye again."

"Look. I didn't do it on purpose. I had no

idea it could squirt so far. Nobody warns you about those things. Hey, do you want to hear a joke Emma told me? What's a pirate's favorite letter of the alphabet?"

"Molly, you're trying to change the subject—"

"You'd think it would be *Arrrr*, but they're really in love with the *C*."

"Molly? You mean it about not getting involved?"

"Oh yes. I mean it. And I really would rather not think about it anymore."

Stephen Park had already benefited from my uncompensated emotional labor while he was alive. He wasn't getting any more from me just because he was dead.

"I only want you to be safe. Both of you." Donnie stood up and went into the walk-in closet. "Are you sure you'll be okay with me going to work today?"

"Fine. Totally back to normal already. Accidents happen."

"You think it was an accident?" Donnie said from inside the closet.

"Probably. But what do I know? It's not

my job to figure out what happened. Like I said, I don't want to think about it."

I flashed back to the sight of Stephen lying lifeless on the ground. I *hoped* it was an accident. If not, someone had just gotten away with murder.

Chapter Nine

MARGARET SHOWED up at exactly two minutes to nine to take over baby duty. Francesca greeted her arrival with a well-timed (from my perspective) diaper explosion. Margaret took the baby from me and went to change her while I settled down at my computer.

One of the persistent myths about academia is that professors get summers "off." Our summers are unpaid, and technically the university can't require us to do anything they're not paying us for.

However. There are things that need to get done, whether it's summer or not. And many of these things fall to the department chair (me).

During the school year, faculty members are supposed to turn in regular reports to the Student Retention Office. These reports don't always get done, because there is no way to force faculty members to take attendance, record student engagement levels, or update their Teaching Philosophy Statements. When the faculty in my department take principled stands against administrative overreach by refusing to fill out the forms, I then have to spend my summer completing the forms myself. Because I had no information to work with, I found myself using the sophisticated data interpolation method known as "making stuff up."

For this course session, please list

a) The date, room assignment, and instructor of record,

b) The current enrollment expressed as a whole integer,

c) The average engagement level on an eleven-point scale, rounded to two decimal places.

d) The average student success level (letter grade on a four-point scale), rounded to two decimal places.

Fortunately for me, the management department was small—only four full-time faculty including me. But multiply that by three or four classes per faculty member times a sixteen-week semester, and it left me with a pile of reports to fill out before fall semester.

I was having some trouble focusing on my task, so when I heard Margaret clear her throat, I welcomed the interruption. I swiveled my chair around to face her.

"Sorry to bother you Professor, but I was wondering if I could ask you something?"

"Sure. Have a seat. Margaret, you can call me Molly. It's been how many years since you were my student?"

She perched on the arm of the couch with Francesca on her lap.

"Sorry, Professor, I guess I'm just used to it. I mean Molly, sorry. I heard about what happened last night. Poor Professor Park. It must have been awful for you."

"Yes. It was. Thank you, Margaret. You're very compassionate."

"You shouldn't feel bad about it, Professor. It's perfectly normal to throw up when you see a dead body. I'm sure everyone understands."

"Margaret, did you have something you wanted to ask me?"

Margaret hitched the baby up onto her shoulder.

"I hate to bother you, but Keola? You know, my boyfriend?"

"I've heard you mention him."

"His job ended, and he's looking for something else. He was working as a lab tech. He has a biology degree. If you know of any opportunities?"

"I can ask around. In fact, Emma Nakamura might know of something. I'll ask her when I see her."

"Thank you so much, Professor. That would be so nice of you!"

"Where was he working before? I know Emma will ask me. She'll want to talk to his previous supervisor."

"Oh, that's the thing." Margaret absently

rubbed the baby's back. "He doesn't feel like he can ask Professor Corcoran for a recommendation."

"Professor Corcoran? Is this Bee Corcoran? In Kinesiology?"

Margaret nodded.

"I see. He doesn't want to bother her while she's grieving. Understandable."

"Grieving?"

"Because Bee and...never mind. Why can't he ask her for a recommendation?"

"She kind of fired him."

"Ah. Do you know why?"

"There was a disagreement about the lab animals. I told him, don't contradict your boss, but I guess he didn't listen."

"Was she mistreating the animals?" Bee could be tactless, but she didn't strike me as someone who tortured helpless creatures.

Margaret shook her head.

"No, it wasn't animal cruelty. You have to report animal cruelty. It was just that Professor Corcoran sometimes got the rats mixed up. Keola would find them in the wrong cages. She didn't want to listen to any of his suggestions for keeping records. I told him, Keola, bosses don't want to hear *your* ideas. They want you to take *their* ideas and make them successful."

"That sounds pretty cynical, Margaret. Where did you hear that?"

"Your Intro to Business Management class."

"Huh. Really?"

"Professor, Keola didn't do anything wrong. He was just trying to help. He loves animals."

"Okay, I'll talk to Emma about it."

"Oh, thank you so much Professor!"

She started to stand up.

"By the way, someone told me you don't get paid in the summer. Is it true?"

"It is true. I'm on a nine-month appointment."

"But you're still working?"

"Yep."

"What are you working on? Sorry, I'm not trying to be nosy. But Keola thinks he might want to be a college professor someday."

Margaret held the baby on her shoulder and swayed rhythmically.

"Sure, I don't mind telling you. Research, prep for fall classes, student petitions, search committees, course scheduling, and whatever's currently on fire in my in-box. Right now, it's paperwork for the Student Retention Office that the other faculty members didn't do during the school year. If I weren't department chair maybe I could take some time off. Travel, or just drop off the face of the earth. Like everyone else in my department seems to be doing."

"So why did you want to become department chair?" Margaret asked.

"I don't know that I *wanted* to. Harrison and Schneider refuse to do it. Every time the dean tries to make them, they threaten to retire. So that leaves Rodge Cowper and me, and I'd rather be department chair than have Rodge be in charge. Sorry, I've probably given you way more information than you wanted."

"No, it's good to know." Margaret stroked Francesca's head, which was resting heavily on her shoulder. "No offense, but honestly? I'm glad I'm going to be an accountant."

Chapter Ten

DONNIE STOPPED in at home after the lunch rush to check on the baby and me. We sat out on the front porch, enjoying the view of Uakoko Street. It had been raining all morning, so the air was pleasantly cool. Donnie fed Francesca from a bottle.

"Well, the news is out," I said. "Margaret already heard all about what happened last night."

"M-hm," Donnie said to Francesca. "Look at her. What a champ. She's not letting that bottle go until she's killed it."

"It's funny," I said. "Francesca's whole world is about consuming the bottle. She's being utterly selfish right now, and it's the most adorable thing imaginable. But imagine a grownup acting the same way. Not adorable at all."

"My customers are a little bit like our baby. They show up, they're hungry and cranky, we feed them, and then they're happy."

"So how are things at work, speaking of your customers? Has anyone asked you about last night?"

"Everyone," Donnie said. "They already knew I was going to the donor dinner because I left work early last night."

"Right. You don't usually take off work."

"People are letting their imaginations go wild."

"What do you mean?"

"Park was relatively young and in pretty good health. And you know, a place like the Old Mahina Memorial Hospital, with its history, people are going to, you know. Assume things."

"Do you mean people think it's haunted?" I asked.

"When you ask people straight out, they say *they* don't believe in ghosts or anything like that. But then they tell you everyone else does."

"Hey, I don't even believe in ghosts, and you wouldn't have a hard time convincing me the old hospital is haunted. Although it is gorgeous. Did you see the ceiling in the dining room?"

Donnie checked his watch and set the baby bottle down on the rattan table. Francesca had fallen asleep in his arms.

"Okay, I have to get back. You two going to be okay?"

I reached out to take Francesca. She woke up and fussed until I popped the bottle back into her mouth.

"We'll be fine," I said. "*Our* house isn't haunted. Also, Emma might stop by later."

"Good. I feel better knowing you have company."

Donnie gave me a quick kiss, and I went back inside. I got Francesca to sleep in her rocking bassinet and was able to answer a few emails before someone rapped on the front door.

"The baby's asleep," I whispered as I let Emma in.

"Nah, she's not," Emma contradicted me. "She's wide awake. Oh, hey little girl!"

"She's awake *now*," I said.

Emma knelt next to the bassinet. Francesca beamed at Emma.

"Aw, she's smiling at me. Look, she wants me to pick her up." Emma picked up the baby. "That okay with you?"

"Sure. Want coffee?"

"Yeah, thanks."

"Want a burp cloth?"

Emma had hoisted the baby onto her shoulder and was marching her around the living room. Francesca giggled and cooed.

"Nah," Emma said. "If she spits up on me I'll just throw my shirt in the wash. Like I did last time."

"Like last time? Oh, you mean you'll make *me* wash it and then you'll take one of my shirts. Oh, before I forget. Can you use a lab tech?"

I told Emma about Margaret's boyfriend.

"You're asking me do I want to hire some little boy who's gonna come in acting like he knows more about running my lab than I do? Yeah, I think I'll pass."

"Well, I told Margaret I'd ask you about it."

"You can tell her I said eff off with that."

"I'll paraphrase."

"Eh, how come she didn't just come ask me? She knows who I am."

"Why didn't the shy, high-strung accounting major approach you directly? I don't know, Emma. It's a mystery. Hey, so I never told you what happened last—"

"Oh yeah, last night! Big news, ah?" Emma was talking to the baby, not to me. "Isn't that *right*, Francesca? Oh, yes, it is."

"Okay, let me go get coffee. You okay watching the baby out here?"

"Auntie Emma wants to hear all about it," I heard Emma tell the baby. "Miss Constance gave mean old Stephen Park what was coming to him, didn't she?"

I brought our coffee back out to the living room.

"Sounds like you heard about Stephen already. What was that you were telling the baby? Emma, don't tell her Stephen Park got what was coming to him. That's not right."

Emma touched her nose to Francesca's.

"Oh, your mommy thinks Aunty Emma's being too mean, but she's wrong, because Stephen totally deserved it, didn't he? I think we need to remind your mommy about the time Stephen forgot all about her birthday because he was too busy—"

"Emma, Stephen might not have been my favorite person, but you can't say someone deserved to die."

"Oh yeah? What about Hitler?"

"Stephen Park was a self-important, faithless poseur, but he wasn't a genocidal dictator."

"As far as you know."

"No, I'm positive he wasn't. He didn't have the initiative."

Emma gave Francesca's chubby cheek a kiss and placed her back in the bassinet. Francesca dropped off to sleep immediately.

"That schmuck broke your heart, Molly. I'm talking about Stephen Park, not Hitler."

Emma examined her shoulder and rubbed the fabric.

"Oh look, baby left me a little blurp. So, tell me from the beginning what happened."

"First you tell me. Who's Miss Constance?"

I handed Emma a coffee mug. She took a sip.

"Mm, I like this one. Good choice, Molly."

"Emma?"

"Oh yeah, Miss Constance. People see her around the old hospital at night sometimes."

"Who is she?" I asked. "I mean, besides a ghost, I got that. But was she a patient? An employee?"

"She was a patient. I heard she was from a rich family and as soon as she got married her husband had her hospitalized for nerves or whatever. Then he went out and partied and spent all her money. You know back in those days that's how it was. Your husband could lock you up in the loony bin and take everything you have and there was nothing you could do about it."

"Yeah, the good old days. So, whatever happened to her?"

"She killed herself," Emma said.

"Oh, how awful."

"Yeah, but she got the last word. Her husband was riding the train—"

"Here? On this island?"

"Yeah, we used to have a train until a bunch of the tracks got washed away by a tsunami. Anyway, his car derailed and fell into the ocean. Him and a bunch of his party buddies were never seen again."

"Wow." I took a sip of my coffee. It had gotten cold. "And people think Constance did it?"

"Uh huh. And that wasn't enough for her. Cause they say she's still around, taking revenge on—"

"Men?" I asked.

"Nah, not all men. Just, you know..." Emma glanced at the sleeping baby.

"Eff-boys," she stage-whispered.

"What boys?"

"Useless idiot party boys," she explained. "You know, like your stepson."

"Ah. Your words, not mine."

"How come I never hear about Davison anymore by the way?" Emma asked.

"Ever since he moved to Vegas he's been too busy to call or visit. It's like he doesn't even exist. It's wonderful."

"Aw, who says there's no happily ever after in real life? Anyway Molly, you were there. Last night. What happened? Tell me everything."

"Okay but first let me put on some fresh coffee. I'll bring out the pot."

Chapter Eleven

"THEY HAD the dining room open to the terrace?" Emma exclaimed.

"You know the layout of the building?" I asked.

"Kinda. Me and my friends used to go exploring there. That terrace is where they say Miss Constance killed herself."

"Ooh. That just gave me a little shiver."

"And now you're telling me Stephen died in the exact same place? Yeah, chicken skin for real. What were they thinking, letting people go out there?"

"It's not like we were encouraged to," I said. "They didn't have any lights on. But they hadn't exactly closed it off, either."

"Why did they have a dinner in the old hospital at all? It's kind of morbid, ah? All those people suffering and dying and losing their minds in there—"

"Oh, but Emma, the building is beautiful."

"Seriously?"

"Inlaid marble floors, big sweeping staircases, there's nothing on the island remotely comparable. I can see why they wanted to have a donor event there, haunted or not."

"They should've at least had lights on." Emma tipped up her mug and then refilled her coffee.

"That reminds me," I said, "Wasn't there supposed to be some big project to catch up on our deferred maintenance and bring all our buildings up to code? Wasn't it part of the deal when the county gave us the building?"

"Old news, Molly. Don't you remember what happened the last legislative session? The ledge zeroed out all our maintenance funding."

"I thought they gave us some money in

the end, though."

"We got three million dollars for football," Emma said. "Everything else got cut."

"Seriously?"

"Seriously."

"See, that's why I don't follow the news. Ugh."

"Molly, that's probably how come they had the donor dinner up there in the first place. So the high maka makas could see for themselves all the work that needs to be done and open up their checkbooks."

"If that was their plan, it backfired. No one was pulling out their checkbooks that night, believe me."

Emma and I drank our coffee in silence for a few moments.

"So, the old hospital building's been closed for decades," I said. "They open it up and the first event they have there, Stephen Park wanders out onto the terrace, the same place where Miss Constance supposedly killed herself, what, a hundred years ago. Next thing you know, he's dead."

"Yeah. Creepy, ah?"

"Ghost stories aside, though. It's not impossible that there was someone up there with Stephen."

"You see or hear anyone?" Emma set down her coffee cup. I lifted it and slid her coaster underneath.

"No. I was just remembering how dark it was out there. Yeah, it was probably an accident. Stephen called my name, and when I didn't answer he leaned too far over the railing and fell."

"Oh yeah, if you hadn't walked by, Stephen wouldn't've tried to get your attention, but you ignored him, so he leaned over to try again, and he fell down. You shouldn't blame yourself for Stephen dying, though."

"It hadn't occurred to me to blame myself, Emma, but thanks ever so much for bringing it up."

"You know, if there wasn't someone else up there with Stephen Park? You're the only one who saw what happened."

"But that's the problem. I didn't see anything. Stephen fell behind me, after I'd already walked past. I only saw him after I heard him fall and turned around."

"You remember anything that happened just before?"

Emma stood up and took our coffee cups into the kitchen.

"Emma, you know what? We should talk about something else. This isn't our problem to solve."

"Sure," Emma called from the kitchen. "As long as you can honestly say you're a hundred percent sure that whoever killed Stephen Park will never kill anyone else."

"Emma, no one killed Stephen Park. Ghost or human. It was an accident."

"Oh yeah? Would you bet your life on it?"

I placed my hands over my eyes, relaxed into the couch cushions, and let my mind float back to that evening. It was a practice I'd learned from Stephen, of all people. Memories want to be found, not forced, he'd said. This technique had never helped me remember my student's names, and it sure hadn't stopped Stephen from forgetting my birthday, but I didn't have any other tricks up my sleeve.

I recalled the glow of Stephen's cigarette and the scent of burning cloves. It was dark, and Stephen had been drinking. No, wait. I was the one who had been drinking. Stephen and Bee had green tea. So, what happened? Either Stephen really wanted to get my attention and lost his balance, or someone had been waiting up there to give him a little shove. Someone who had been pushed to his limit.

I moved my hands off my eyes and pressed my fingers into my temples.

"Got some fresh coffee…" I heard the clunk of cups on the bare wood of the coffee table, but I couldn't will myself to open my eyes, much less do anything about it.

The couch cushion jumped as Emma plunked down next to me.

"Ooh, Molly, you okay? Got one of those ice cream headaches?"

"Ice *pick* headaches," I groaned. "Ice cream. I should be so lucky. Okay. I think it's gone."

I slowly released the pressure on my temples, opened my eyes, and sat up.

"What aren't you telling me?" Emma demanded.

"What do you mean? I'm telling you everything." I avoided looking at her and concentrated on putting coasters under the coffee mugs.

"I know you, Molly. You only get those headaches when you get da kine. Too many ideas in your head fighting with each other."

"Cognitive dissonance." I picked up my cup and held it under my nose. The coffee aroma made me feel a little better. "Emma. Do you think Donnie is jealous?"

"Of what?"

"Not *of* something," I said. "I mean is he jealous in general. Like Othello."

"The 'who's on first' guy?"

"Donnie was not happy about having to sit with Stephen."

"Molly, what guy would want to have dinner with his wife's ex?"

"I know. Maybe I'm overthinking it. Is the baby still asleep?".

Emma leaned over the arm of the couch to check.

"Uh-huh. She's out."

"Good. Thanks. You know, I'll be honest. I wasn't thrilled about having to sit there either."

"Oh yeah, having to sit next to Bee the Body right after you had a baby? I don't blame you."

"Bee the Body? Who calls her Bee the Body?"

"Everyone," Emma replied. "You gotta admit, she's hot."

"I guess, if you buy into Eurocentric, ageist, thinness-privileging—"

"So in other words, you admit she's hot."

"It's not fair. That low level of body fat is completely unattainable for...most women."

"Oh, you thinking *Donnie* killed Stephen Park?" Emma said.

"No, I I'm not saying I think Donnie did it. It's just—"

"Then look me in the eye instead of talking to your coffee."

I set my mug down and angled myself to face Emma.

"Stephen was really getting under Donnie's skin that night. I could tell."

"Yeah, Stephen's annoying. No argument there. But Molly, Donnie is not a hothead. When has he ever made an impulsive decision? Besides marrying you."

"He made a point of asking me not to investigate Stephen's murder. I hadn't even mentioned investigating anything. Why would he do that?"

"Cause he knows you like to go poking your nose into things, and he doesn't want some crazy idiot shoving you into a lava tube and leaving him widowed with a baby to take care of."

"Why does everyone keep bringing up the stupid lava tube incident? I make one little mistake—"

"What about Stephen's ex-girlfriends?" Emma interrupted. "You know if anyone was stalking him?"

"I don't know about his ex-girlfriends. I don't get involved in Stephen's personal affairs."

"What? How about the girl he was

cheating on you with? You broke 'em up, don't forget."

"I did nothing of the kind. All I did was let it slip that Stephen Park was not, in fact, part-Korean."

"And she dropped him like a maggot sandwich."

"Wow, what a disgusting expression."

"But accurate. Eh, sounds like Donnie's home."

"I don't think so. This is peak lunch hour at the Drive-Inn. Besides, it doesn't sound like Donnie's car."

Chapter Twelve

DETECTIVE KA`IMI Medeiros strode into the living room, the floorboards straining under his weight. His demeanor alone would have been intimidating enough, even if he had been the size of an ordinary man, which he wasn't. His aloha shirt could have doubled as a slipcover for one of our armchairs.

Emma, the coward, quickly made her excuses and skedaddled, leaving the baby and me alone with the plainclothes Goliath.

I offered Medeiros a cup of coffee. He refused.

"Did you want to talk to Donnie? He should be down at the Drive-Inn." I took my seat on the end of the couch next to the baby's bassinet. Medeiros carefully lowered himself onto one of the aforementioned armchairs.

"Actually, I was hoping to ask you a few questions, Professor. About the events leading up to Stephen Park's death."

"Oh. Wonderful. Okay. You did get my statement that night. Was there more?"

Medeiros reached into his shirt pocket and took out a tiny notepad and pencil.

"Just following up on a few details. Can you describe the interaction between your husband and Stephen Park prior to your discovery of Park's body?"

Was this the part where I was supposed to clam up and demand a lawyer? No, that would have been silly. A lawyer for what? I wasn't in trouble.

"Civil, I suppose? I guess it's no secret Stephen Park and I used to date."

"No. It's pretty well-known."

"Oh, good."

"To your knowledge did your husband have any conflict with the deceased?"

"Donnie gets along with everyone," I said.

"It didn't bother him that you had been in a romantic relationship with Park?"

"It was over before I even met Donnie."

"But is it possible there was still some jealousy?"

Ouch. I had to hand it to Medeiros. Despite having been friends with Donnie since elementary school or whenever, he wasn't shying away from the hard questions.

"Detective, Donnie is a devoted husband and father, an honorable businessman, and an outstanding human being. Stephen Park was a narcissist, a predator, a fraud, and Donnie's inferior in every possible way. Donnie had absolutely no reason to be jealous of Stephen Park."

Medeiros wrote in his notebook for what seemed like a long time.

"How about you, Professor?" he said finally.

"Me?"

"How did you get along with Stephen Park?"

"Fine, I guess."

"Can you be more specific?"

"I mean, I didn't socialize with him. But I saw him now and then around campus. He was the theater department chair, and I'm the chair of the management department in the College of Commerce. Mostly I'd run into him at department chair meetings."

"You called him a predator," Medeiros said. "Why?"

"Oh, that. He dated students."

Whimpering sounds came from Francesca's bassinet.

"Would you excuse me, please?"

"Yes, of course," he said.

I picked up the baby and the nursing pillow and took a seat on the chair next to my computer. With my back to Medeiros, I got Francesca latched on. All the action was hidden under my baggy t-shirt, so there would be no possibility of indecent exposure.

"How did your relationship with Stephen Park end?" Medeiros asked as I swiveled to face him. His eyes flicked briefly to the baby legs sticking out from the bottom of my shirt, but his expression remained neutral.

"We went our separate ways," I said.

He held his pen above his notepad and waited.

"He stood me up on my birthday," I said, finally. "He claimed he'd lost track of time, and I found out later that he'd been with, yes, one of his students. But it was a long time ago, Detective. I've moved on. I mean, look at me. I'm married with a baby. The whole situation with Stephen Park, it's over. It's not something I dwell on."

He nodded and wrote on his tiny notepad.

"And the worst thing about it was," I continued, "Stephen wasn't even a little bit contrite. The fact that he left me waiting for him, on my birthday, was my fault somehow. Like *I* was being unreasonable for expecting him to keep his appointments or something. Because *his* time was valuable, and mine wasn't."

"How did your husband feel about the fact that you had contact with Stephen Park at your workplace?"

"I don't think it bothered him. I doubt he ever gave it a thought."

Underneath my shirt Francesca squirmed and tugged. I tried not to grimace.

"In your view, is it possible that your husband, if provoked, might have gotten into an altercation with the deceased?"

"Detective, you know how even-tempered Donnie is. He's the last person in the world who would get pulled into some chest-thumping nature-show display with his wife's ex. Now if you're looking for someone with a motive to kill Stephen Park—"

Just as I was hitting my stride, I heard the garage door open. Donnie was home. Lunch rush at Donnie's Drive-Inn must have ended early. The sound made Francesca fussy. I struggled to get her calmed down while she did her best to rip my nipple from its moorings. Medeiros kept his eyes on his notepad.

"Donnie, hi!" I said as he came into the living room. "Look who stopped by for a chat!"

Medeiros stood, and they greeted each

other with a hand grip. Donnie was almost as tall as Ka`imi Medeiros, but Medeiros beat Donnie hands-down in the width department.

"Coffee," Donnie offered.

"Thanks, ah?"

Donnie went to the kitchen to make coffee and Medeiros sat back down. Why had Medeiros accepted coffee from Donnie, but not from me? The man had never trusted me, that I knew, but did he think I was going to poison him?

"Who do you think had a motive to kill Stephen Park?" Medeiros asked as I wrangled the squirmy baby.

"Well, let me say straight off that I don't want to speak ill of the dead." Like any good Catholic, I know you're supposed to make that disclaimer before you launch into speaking ill of the dead. "But as I mentioned, Stephen did have a habit of getting involved with his students. I'll bet there are a few angry parents out there that you might want to talk to."

Medeiros nodded.

"You already mentioned Stephen Park

dating his students. Any particular individuals I should follow up with?"

This was where a better memory for names would have come in handy.

"There was an Alyson. No, Alicia?"

"Last name?"

"I'm sorry, I don't remember."

Donnie came in with two cups of coffee on a tray with a cream pitcher and a sugar bowl.

"I can go into the back room if you want to talk out here," I said. Donnie declined my offer, so I wouldn't have to pick up the baby and move. Instead, the men went out to the lanai. I stayed indoors, nursed the baby, and watched cat videos on my computer. Then I went to bed early.

Chapter Thirteen

I WAS asleep by the time Donnie came to bed, and I didn't have much luck the next morning trying to find out what Medeiros had asked about. I followed him into the bathroom, hoping to get him to talk.

"So what did you two talk about last night?" I asked. "You were out there for a while."

"Nothing too interesting," Donnie said.

"Did Medeiros tell you how Stephen died?"

"You know Ka`imi. He doesn't tell you much."

"So, what did he ask you?"

"Just the normal things. Probably the

same questions he asked you. Right, Francesca?"

I held Francesca so she could watch Donnie shave. She stared at him with big eyes as he leaned into the bathroom mirror and ran an electric razor over the lower half of his face. He stood up, tapped the razor against the sink, then rinsed it and wiped it down. All of this fascinated the baby.

Then he turned around, kissed the top of my head, bent down to kiss the baby's chubby cheek, told us he'd see us for lunch, and headed out to work.

I decided to use the time between Donnie's departure and Margaret's arrival to take a walk. It was still cool outside, so it would be pleasant for Francesca as well as good weight-bearing exercise for me.

I trudged uphill toward the dead end of the street and reviewed the events of the past two days. The fact that Medeiros was asking questions meant that Stephen's death wasn't considered an accident. And I didn't like what he was asking about Donnie and Stephen. It was one thing for me to wonder what Donnie might be capable of. But for

Medeiros to suspect Donnie seemed paranoid and wrong of him.

A car went past, and I stepped off the road onto a neighbor's lawn. I liked my little street, but sometimes I missed the big-city amenities. Like sidewalks, streetlights, and roads wide enough to fit two cars at once. Fortunately, traffic was sparse, and my neighbors didn't seem to mind the occasional pedestrian on their lawn.

I stepped back onto the asphalt and resumed stewing about Detective Medeiros.

Maybe Medeiros didn't believe I'd tell the truth on my own and assumed he had to rattle me. To shake loose whatever I might have been keeping to myself. Medeiros has always mistrusted me, ever since the first time Emma and I found ourselves accidentally mixed up in a murder case. Neither of us had ever wanted to get involved. Every time it happened it was because of some weird chain of coincidences that no one could have predicted. But as any hard-boiled detective novel will tell you, men like Ka`imi Medeiros don't believe in coincidence.

Or maybe Medeiros's suspicions had nothing to do with me. Maybe someone put the idea in his head, about Donnie being jealous of Stephen. But who? There was Geoffrey "Chaucer" Gunderson, the arts and sciences dean. He sat with us long enough to have perceived the tension at our table. And the young woman who came by with the tea and wine, who wouldn't look Stephen in the eye (and vice versa). It didn't take much imagination to guess what was going on there. The poor girl must have been one of Stephen's discarded conquests. But what possible reason would either of them have to direct suspicion toward Donnie?

Then there was Bee Corcoran. Maybe she was so upset at losing Stephen that she was looking for someone to blame. Or maybe she had a more sinister motivation for misdirecting Detective Medeiros? No, I was letting my imagination get ahead of the evidence now. I stopped to readjust the baby carrier and work the kink out of my back. I had hoped to get in shape by carrying the baby around, but she was gaining weight much faster than I was gaining strength.

Stephen's death was an accident, I told myself. Medeiros would poke around and disrupt people's lives for a while until he figured it out, and then everything would go back to normal. It was highly unlikely that there was a murderer on the loose.

It occurred to me then that I should reach out to Bee Corcoran. Just to see how she was holding up in the aftermath of Stephen's death. Bee hadn't been at Mahina State that long, and as far as I could tell, Stephen was her only friend there. From what Stephen had told me, Bee was estranged from her family. A friendly call from a coworker wouldn't be amiss at a time like this. Of course, I wouldn't ask Bee any inappropriate questions, like what she remembered from the night of Stephen's death, or who might have wanted to kill him. That would be bad form. But if she wanted to talk things through with a sympathetic colleague, I'd be there to listen. She'd even given me her phone number and told me to call any time if I had questions about getting my pre-pregnancy body back. Why would she have given me her number if she didn't want me to call her?

I'd be doing Bee a kindness by calling. A mitzvah, as Emma would say.

I took out my phone and turned my back to the sun so I could see the screen. Francesca watched, fascinated, as I dialed Bee's number. While the phone rang I debated how I would start the conversation. Bee picked up the phone before I could decide.

"Hey Molly," she said.

"Oh. You knew it was me calling?"

"The Caller ID gave you away. How are you holding up? Are you taking care of yourself?"

Darn it, she's got me off balance already. I was going to ask *her* how she was doing.

"I'm fine," I said. "Taking a walk with the baby. How are you?"

"I can't pretend everything's okay, but this grant report is keeping me busy. Oh yeah, and I had to fire one of my student workers."

We spent a few minutes trading student

worker horror stories. Then a pause in the conversation gave me the opportunity to introduce a new topic.

"Has Detective Medeiros talked to you?" I asked. "About what happened?"

"Medeiros?"

"He's a big, tall guy, maybe forties or early fifties, short black hair, he was wearing a red aloha shirt with a yellow taro leaf print?"

"Oh, yes, of course. I remember him. He was great. So friendly and comforting."

"What?"

"It was one of the worst nights of my life and he really put me at ease."

"Are we still talking about Detective Medeiros?"

"I can't believe it, Molly. Stephen's really gone."

"It is kind of surreal," I agreed.

Francesca and I had reached the top of the street. Although it was not yet nine o'clock, the sun was shining hot, and my belly was sweating where the baby carrier covered it. I adjusted the baby's hat to shade her face, turned toward the sun, and started back down to the house.

"Detective Medeiros doesn't think Stephen's death was an accident," I said.

"What do you mean?"

Medeiros hadn't sworn me to secrecy or anything. I couldn't think of any reason why I shouldn't tell Bee about my interview with him.

"He was asking me about Donnie's, my husband's, interaction with Stephen that night. You didn't see anything, did you? No raised voices or anything like that?"

"Well...I mean, it's totally understandable," Bee said.

"What's understandable?"

"Your husband not being crazy about Stephen. I mean, what guy wants to sit across the table from his wife's ex?"

Why did she assume it was Donnie who disliked Stephen? Donnie had been patient and gracious throughout the whole ordeal, while Stephen had pouted and snarked like a middle-schooler. But Bee apparently remembered things differently.

"I'm *Stephen's* ex," I pointed out. "And you

don't seem to have any animosity toward me. What's so funny?"

"Stephen and I were friends," she said, suppressing her laughter. "But I would never…I mean, that was all. We weren't romantically involved. I can't even imagine…I'm sorry, I shouldn't laugh. It's not funny. I'm sorry. I don't mean to disrespect the dead."

"It's okay. You have a lovely laugh." It was true, she did. Just the right mixture of throaty and silvery. "Wait. You and Stephen weren't a thing?"

"No. You can have a male friend without it being a 'thing', can't you?"

"Well, sure. I mean, I'm friends with Pat Flanagan. You don't know him—"

"The news blogger? Island Confidential?"

"Yes. That's him. Okay, I guess you do know him."

"Just from reading the blog. His haunted Hawaii stories are great. I'd love to meet him sometime."

"Sure. So, really? You and Stephen

weren't an item? He seemed to think pretty highly of you."

The few times I'd run into Stephen over the past semester, he'd unfailingly brought the conversation around to the topic of Dr. Bee Corcoran and her amazing awesomeness. Bee, according to Stephen, was a triathlete, a fitness model (which I gather is like a regular model but with even less bodyfat), and a research superstar. Stephen would never fail to mention how *brave* Bee was to claim the life she wanted for herself, and how despite "everything," she was the most *feminine* woman he'd ever met.

Why hadn't I noticed that Stephen had been getting more muscular? Because I had been trying my best to ignore him. It was only at the dinner that I'd been forced to look at him for any length of time.

"No. I told you, we were buds, that's all. Besides, it was pretty clear he still wasn't over you, Molly."

"He...what?"

"I mean, I guess I can understand why

you dumped him for Donnie, but honestly? He had a hard time accepting it."

I sputtered for a moment and finally managed to form words.

"*I* dumped *him*...is *that* what he told you?"

"I guess it doesn't matter now, sad to say. Hey Molly, did you remember to drink your lemon water this morning?"

"Not yet." I was barely paying attention to what Bee was saying. I was furious at Stephen for selling Bee his preposterous story with himself as the wronged hero. And me as the heartless villain, or course. But if I tried to set the record straight now, I would just sound petty.

"Just one glass of lemon water in the morning," Bee said. "It'll keep you from overeating."

"Right. I remember."

"Don't worry, Molly, you'll lose that baby fat. Just keep at it."

"Thanks, Bee. So glad I called."

Chapter Fourteen

I HAD BEEN LOOKING FORWARD to my usual late lunch with Donnie, but after Margaret left, he called home to cancel.

"We're slammed," he explained. "The lunch rush usually dies down by now. Not today."

"Oh. But that's good, right?"

"If people were only showing up to buy lunch, yes, it would be. But I think a lot of people are here because of the...incident. Word's getting out that I was at the dinner when Park died. And people are asking me about it. It's a little uncomfortable, to tell you the truth."

I'd become accustomed to the Mahina rumor mill, aka the Coconut Wireless. It used to bother me, but I've long since given up on any expectation of privacy.

"Rubberneckers?" I asked.

"You mean like people who slow down to stare at a car accident? Exactly. That's the feeling I'm getting from a lot of them."

"But are they buying food?"

"I suppose so."

"Doesn't seem like a problem to me then. Let me rephrase that. It seems like a silver lining to an otherwise tragic situation. Want me to write you some talking points?"

"No, it's fine. I'll be okay. I just wanted to let you know what was going on. You two stay safe, okay?"

"Listen, Donnie, I was talking to Bee Corcoran this morning—"

"Molly, I'm sorry, I have to get going. I'll see you tonight. Love you both."

I wanted to talk to someone besides the baby. I called Emma to see whether she could come over.

A few minutes after I hung up, Emma knocked on the door.

"I'm glad you called, Molly," Emma swept in and made a beeline for the refrigerator. "I gotta talk to someone who understands. In other words, not Yoshi. You know they say the only thing worse than being married to another academic is being married to a non-academic. You got any beer?"

"Just wine. Can you pour me one too? And a big glass of water while you're there?"

"Water? Oh yeah, the baby. Okay, sit down. I'll be right there."

Emma brought three big mugs out to the living room, set two of them down in front of me, then sat down and took a big gulp from hers.

"I'll go first," she said. "Friggin' Bee Corcoran."

"Bee Corcoran! That's funny, I just... what about Bee?"

"I think Gunderson's gonna nominate her research for the system life sciences award." Emma narrowed her eyes. "Which means I'm out."

"But Emma, your research...I mean, I'm not an expert, but what you're doing seems really important. To the environment and everything. Right?"

"That's what I thought." Emma lifted the mug to her mouth and kept tilting it back and drinking until it was upside-down.

"Is it just one nomination per campus?" I asked.

"Uh-huh."

"Ohhh. Hm. I saw Geoffrey Gunderson at the dinner. I think he did say he nominated Bee."

Silence fell over my living room.

"I need another glass," Emma said, finally. "You?"

"I'm fine."

I waited for her to come back from the kitchen.

"You've been spending years on it, haven't you?" I said. "Mapping the family trees of native plant species, right?"

Emma lifted her mug in a mock toast.

"Yeah, pretty much. Not bad for an English major, Molly."

"I'll take it. So, what's Bee doing that's more impressive than what you're doing?"

Emma set down her mug.

"You know about DNA, right?"

"Yes, I do, thank you for asking. That's what you study, yes?"

"Yeah. I study plant DNA. But us humans have DNA too."

"Emma, I'm not a complete moron. Plus, I've seen GATTACA. I know humans have DNA."

"Sorry about assuming you're a moron, Molly. I've been spending too much time talking to administrators, that's why. Like my dean."

"Come on, Emma, Geoffrey Gunderson seems perfectly nice."

"Have you ever tried to explain gene mapping to a medievalist?"

"I have not. Go ahead and tell me about DNA."

"Okay." Emma set down her wine mug. "You know how your eye color, earwax, stuff like that is determined by your DNA, right?"

"Earwax?"

"Yeah. You probably have wet earwax."

"How would you know that?"

"Don't get distracted when I'm trying to explain stuff. Look. Muscle, right?" Emma held her arm up and tapped her meaty bicep. "You know how you work out, you grow more muscle?"

"Theoretically, yes."

"So you have these processes in your body that work to build muscle, yeah? But how come your muscles don't just keep growing and growing forever?"

"Well, there must be some natural limit—"

"Ha! Exactly. So these other processes that keep the growth under control, so you don't grow too much muscle. That's what Bee's researching."

"Oh. So if you're a bodybuilder, you'd want to find out what's keeping your muscles from getting as big as possible, right?"

"Yes."

"And you'd want to slow down or stop that process."

Emma pointed at me.

"Exactly. And not just bodybuilders. If

you can get a handle on the mechanism, you can treat people with muscle wasting conditions."

"She can't be the only one working on that," I said. "There must be a huge market for a treatment like what you're describing."

"That's the thing. People have been trying to crack this for years. But somehow, apparently, she's finally nailed it. Molly, how can I compete with that?"

Francesca had dozed off, so I set her down into the bassinet. She immediately woke up and started fussing. I slid the bassinet next to me and rocked it gently with my foot, which seemed to calm her down again.

"Has Bee actually published anything?" I asked. "About this research, I mean? Maybe it's just vaporware."

Emma pointed at me again.

"Exactly! It has not been peer-reviewed."

"Interesting."

"She presented it at a conference, and it got a bunch of publicity. I'm surprised you didn't hear about it, Molly."

I looked down at Francesca, who was starting to stir.

"I've been a little busy," I said. Then something struck me.

"Stephen!" I exclaimed.

"What about him?" Emma asked.

"When I saw him, he looked like he'd been working out."

Emma snorted.

"Stephen Park? Isn't he way too cool to go to the gym and sweat in front of everyone?"

"Exactly. But he was definitely more muscular than I'd ever seen him. He had the shoulders and everything. Do you think he was Bee's guinea pig?"

"What? Testing a treatment like that on human subjects? Aw, no way. She'd never get that approved. Our IRB doesn't let us do bupkis."

"What if it wasn't approved," I said, "but she did it anyway? Think about it. You know how Stephen is about his appearance. Was. He was so self-conscious when he gained weight after rehab."

"I guess," Emma said. "I don't think I

would've noticed, except when he started wearing capes to cover it up."

"Maybe Stephen found out something about Bee's research," I said, "and was going to make it public. So she had to stop him."

"Ooh, are you saying she killed him?"

"No, Emma, I don't know. I'm just brainstorming."

"Nah, I like it. Go on."

"Okay. Maybe she was doing something unethical, or at least something the IRB didn't approve in advance. Maybe she was experimenting on Stephen, and he consented at first, but then he got some side effects and changed his mind. Oh, great, she's awake."

I picked up Francesca and popped her under my shirt. She latched on right away. I was getting good at this. I was also suddenly desperately thirsty.

"Emma, can you get me another glass of water?"

"What? Oh, sure."

Emma disappeared into the kitchen and returned with a big tumbler.

"Your idea's a little out there," Emma

said as she handed me the glass. "But I can see it. If someone didn't kill him then the only other explanations are either he fell on accident or Miss Constance got him."

"It was so weird to see Stephen Park looking like he'd been lifting weights," I said. "I was like, when did you turn into such a basic bro?"

"Eh, there's nothing wrong with lifting weights." Emma plunked down on an armchair. "You should try it."

"Try it? Hey, I'm lifting weights all day, every day." I looked down at the baby latched to my chest. "Boy, I hope she doesn't grow up to be like Stephen. You know, Stephen's parents aren't bad people. And his sister's perfectly nice. But Stephen. How does someone grow up to be so entitled and arrogant?"

"Stephen was spoiled, that's why. He always got everything he wanted."

"Ah, that reminds me. Not everything. When I talked to Bee this morning—"

"You what?"

"Yeah, I called her. Anyway, she told me

she and Stephen were just friends. No romance."

"What? Nah." Emma leaned forward, interested. "Maybe he was trying to get jacked to impress Bee then."

"Maybe? It seems unlike him to make that much of an effort."

"So, let's flesh out our theory." Emma leaned back into the chair and folded her hands behind her head. "Stephen is using Bee's treatment to get all jacked. He might be the first human subject to try it."

"He'd be all over that," I said. "He loves to think of himself as a risk-taker."

"Okay, but then he starts to get some bad side effects. He tells her to fix it. She says sorry, she can't. He gets upset and threatens to report her. She knows she can't let that happen. So she acts all nice to him, that way he won't get suspicious. But the whole time she's waiting for an opportunity, yeah? When he goes outside for a smoke, she sees her chance. She sneaks out after him and shoves him off the terrace. Then she comes back in, and pretends to be surprised when she hears the news."

"Sounds plausible to me," I said.

"She could've sent 'im over with one push, too," Emma said. "You seen her arms, yeah?"

"Oh yes. She was wearing a sleeveless top at the dinner. She looked like a golden statue of Athena come to life. It was appalling."

"So we solved it. Bee killed Stephen Park to keep her secret safe."

"If I didn't know better, I'd think you wanted Bee to be guilty of murder so she won't get the research award."

"It was your idea to begin with, Molly. Anyway, you don't know what it feels like to lose that research award."

"True, because I've never had a research award. They don't really expect us to bring in grant money in the College of Commerce."

"Man, why didn't I become a business professor?"

"Because it would be so contrary to your nature that your every waking minute would be a torment of self-loathing?"

"Yeah, something like that. Molly, I'm gonna get more wine. You want some?"

"Not right now, thanks," I said. "But could you refill my water?"

Chapter Fifteen

EMMA'S FEARS about the research award were confirmed a few days later. A university-wide email from the chancellor's office announced that the system life sciences award had been granted to Dr. Beatrice Corcoran of Mahina State University for her research on muscle metabolism.

I heard the news first from Emma. She called while Donnie was home for lunch. I invited her to come over. She accepted.

"Emma." Donnie half-stood to give Emma a careful hug without tipping the baby out of the sling. "Congratulations. I heard Mahina State won the system life sciences award. You beat out all the other campuses."

I was shaking my head at Donnie and mouthing the word "no" at him, but he didn't see me until it was too late.

Emma pushed him away and stormed into the kitchen.

"No congratulate me, bradda. Molly, you explain."

I was glad we didn't have a door between the dining room and the kitchen. Because if there had been a door, Emma would have slammed it.

"Emma thought she had a shot at that award," I said quietly."

Donnie's face fell.

"Sorry," he whispered.

"Eh, no need whisper, you two," Emma called from inside the kitchen. "I may be washed-up useless deadwood, but I'm not deaf."

"She shouldn't take it personally," Donnie whispered even more quietly.

"What was that?" Emma yelled. "No secrets, ah?"

"It's hard not to take it personally," I

replied. "It was up to each dean to pick the nominee for their campus. So she can't even blame some faceless committee on Oahu. Emma's own dean backed Bee's research and not Emma's. And get this, Bee claims she didn't even apply. Gunderson thought Bee's research was so impressive he put in the application for her."

"That's right." Emma burst back into the room, holding my sixteen-ounce Chicken Boy coffee mug. She pulled out the chair next to Donnie and plunked down into it. "That's who chose the 'most promising or impactful life science research at the university.' A frickin' medieval studies professor with holes in his sweater and his glasses on his forehead who couldn't tell Gregor Mendel from Josef Mengele."

"Emma, Gunderson wears an aloha shirt like everyone else. Where does the sweater with the holes in it come from?"

Emma took a long drink instead of answering me.

"You're just throwing around random humanities professor stereotypes, aren't you?" I asked. "Is that wine?"

"It's water. Ha! Just kidding. It's gin."

"Straight gin?" Donnie asked.

"Nah. I put ice in it." Emma moved the mug back and forth, so we could hear the ice clink. "Come on. I'm not an animal."

"By the way, Emma, it wasn't Gunderson who didn't know the difference between Mendel and Mengele. It was Linda from the Student Retention Office. Don't you remember? You emailed the whole campus about it."

Donnie glanced at his watch.

"Do you have to get back?" I asked.

"Pretty soon. Francesca's sleeping so nicely. I don't want to disturb her."

"Not that I don't respect Bee," Emma said. "I mean, right now I hate her guts of course, but she's doing a heck of a job promoting herself and picking a sexy research topic. How can mapping plant genomes compete against inventing a magic muscle pill? Man. I guess I knew this was coming. But it still hurts."

Francesca whimpered in her sleep. Donnie stood up carefully.

"I'll change her and put her in her crib," he said.

"Thanks!" I called after him.

Emma took another swig from the mug.

"Just between you and me, Molly? I think it's shibai."

"What is?"

"This whole thing. Gunderson promoting her research. Her acting like it's a big surprise, like who, little old me? There's gotta be some kind of gaming the system going on."

"You really think so? Or are you just saying all this because you're mad and you hate Bee's guts?"

"Nah, Molly. I've been looking into the research and where it's at now. Number one, Bee's results are really preliminary. She doesn't even have any *in vivo* studies published yet. Number two, no one's been able to get close to where the press release says Bee is. What are the chances someone at Mahina State is suddenly gonna crack the code when researchers at the top universities and the big pharma companies haven't been able to?"

"To be fair, the big pharma companies can't develop every possible drug. The approval process takes so long that they need to bring out profitable drugs that people take for their entire lives. Like cholesterol drugs. If Bee's muscle treatment is just going to be used by hardcore bodybuilders and people with rare diseases, it won't bring in enough money to cover their initial investment."

"Oh, so now you're the big expert on the pharmaceutical industry?"

"I wouldn't say I'm an expert, but I do know something about—"

"I guess anyone can be an expert these days, ah?" Emma interrupted. "Like Geoffrey Gunderson, sitting in front of his fireplace, sucking on his pipe and deciding whose life science research is the most impactful."

"You gave him a fireplace and a pipe now?"

Emma rattled the ice in her mug, frowned at it, and took another gulp.

"Anyway," I said, "the pharma example is

from one of the cases I use in my Intro to Business Management class."

"Fine, blah blah blah business reasons. Still doesn't explain how come someone at another university hasn't done it yet."

"Good point. So, you say you examined the research. Do you have any evidence that Bee faked her results?"

Donnie came back out, wiping his hands on a paper towel.

"Faked results? That escalated quickly." He came over and gave me a kiss. "Francesca's changed and asleep. I'm going back. See you tonight. Bye, Emma."

"Laters." Emma watched him leave and then turned to me. "Molly, the more I think about it, the more I'm sure I'm right. There's no way Bee's research is as far along as she says."

"Do you mean, the more you stew about it the more you want to do something to get back at Bee? Emma, if you want to blame someone, blame Gunderson. He put in the application for her, and then he picked her application to forward to the system."

Emma set her cup down harder than necessary and pointed at me.

"Exactly. Favoritism. Predetermined outcome. The whole thing stinks."

"But it worked, didn't it? Out of all the campuses in the system, we got the award. When was the last time Mahina got the system life sciences award?"

"Let's see. The last time we got it was...never."

"So, it sounds like Gunderson made a smart—"

"That's it," Emma declared. "I'm gonna blow the whistle."

I reached over and slid the mug away from Emma. Too late. It was almost empty.

"Emma. Blow the whistle on what, exactly?"

"Are you saying I should keep my mouth shut?" Emma challenged me.

"No, I'm saying don't go accusing people unless you have actual evidence. It's one thing to sit around and spin wild stories, but...look, what if you're wrong, and Bee's discovered something that works? It would alleviate suffering and might even bring the university some income. Imagine, we could travel to conferences. Get the air conditioning working. Finally fix that leaky toxic waste storage shed next to your building, or whatever that thing is. Emma, this could be good."

Emma grabbed back the Chicken Boy mug and glared at me.

"Molly, you are not being a good friend right now."

"What do you want me to say? If you have evidence of fraud you should report it. Otherwise, let Bee do her thing and bring our university money and glory."

Emma stared into her mug.

"It's not right, Molly. That's all I'm saying. It's not right."

Chapter Sixteen

A RINGING SOUND INTERRUPTED US. I looked at Emma, and she looked at me.

"That's not my ringtone," I said.

Emma shrugged. "Mine either. Don't you have a landline?"

"Oh, that's right. We do. No one ever calls it, though." I pushed the chair back and sprinted to the computer desk in the corner of the living room.

The handset Caller ID flashed a 310-prefix number that I didn't recognize at first.

"Probably a junk call. Hello?" I expected to hear a recorded voice imploring me to call for important information about my car's extended warranty. Like anyone would sell an extended warranty on a 1959 Thunderbird.

"Is this Molly?"

There was no mistaking the bracing Brooklyn accent.

"Tiffany! Ohhh, wow!" I tried to disguise the panic in my voice as enthusiasm. *Stephen's mother*, I mouthed to Emma. She grimaced. Not because she had anything against Stephen's mother, but because she knows how adept I am at negotiating delicate, emotionally-fraught situations.

"Tiffany, how are you? I'm sorry, I shouldn't ask how you're doing. Not good, of course, how could you be? What am I saying? Poor Stephen. I can't imagine…"

Emma shook her head and took the mug back into the kitchen.

"Oh Molly, it's awful," Stephen's mother said. "Just awful. *You* must be absolutely devastated!"

Stephen's parents had been convinced that Stephen and I were going to get married. Even after our breakup, which they seemed to believe was a temporary bump in the road.

"Och, Molly!" Stephen's father, Angus Park, was on the phone now. "How are ye holdin' up?"

Stephen's father sounded even more Scottish than the last time I'd talked to him. This despite his having lived in Los Angeles for decades.

"Angus, I am so sorry. I can't even imagine. Is there anything at all I can do?"

"Well we'd love to see you," Stephen's mother said.

"Yes, of course, me too. But I don't think I'll have the chance to travel to California anytime soon—"

"Oh, Molly, I'm not talking about coming out to California," Stephen's mother said. "We're here,"

"You're here? You mean you're here in Mahina?"

Emma was on her way back from the kitchen. She nearly dropped her drink but managed to set it on the table just in time.

"Aye," said Stephen's father. "An I don't mind telling ye, it's no what we expected."

"It's like the third world here, is what he means," Stephen's mother added. "I guess you're not supposed to say that now. I don't mean it in a bad way. It's just the kind of thing Stephen would have liked, isn't it, Angus? But the hotel is pretty primitive."

"Where are you staying?" I asked. "I can recommend a place if you like."

"It's called the Lehua Inn." Stephen's mother pronounced it "Le-hwa."

"Oh. Sorry, that's pretty much our nicest hotel."

"Can we come now? Give us your address and we'll punch it into the GPS. We'd invite you to meet us here, but they won't let us check in yet. You're not near the lava, are you?"

"No, we're nowhere near the lava flow. But really, you don't have to—"

"Oh, what am I thinking? I have your address right here."

"You do?"

"Stephen had you as his local emergency contact. Okay, we'll be over in a few minutes."

I replaced the phone and came back over to sit with Emma.

"Stephen's parents are coming here," I said.

"Yeah, I heard the whole thing."

"And he had me as his local emergency contact. Why me?"

She slid her mug over and I took a big gulp. Which I quickly regretted.

"Warm gin?" I sputtered.

"The ice was diluting it too much. Molly, Stephen's parents like you a lot, ah? It's weird. How come they like you so much?"

"My delightful personality and sterling moral character. What a ridiculous question."

"Nah, for real though."

"I think they liked the way I'd clean up Stephen's messes. And the fact that I'm the daughter of a prominent OB-GYN. Also, I'm not underage."

"Bee's not underage."

"Bee's not his girlfriend."

"When you put it that way, I guess you do look pretty good on paper. Do they know you're married and have a kid?"

"I don't know. I haven't been in touch with them. Who knows what Stephen told them?"

"I bet he let them believe what they wanted to believe. What if they think you're the bereaved fiancée? Someone should let them know, Molly."

"You're right. Someone should. I wish it didn't have to be me."

I heard Francesca fussing in the bedroom and went back to see what she wanted. I had just brought her back out and gotten her latched on when the phone rang again. Emma brought the handset over to me.

"Molly." It was Stephen's mother again. "We're trying to find your house, but the GPS has us next to a big graveyard."

"Yes, that's right." I harbored a wild hope that this would put them off. "I am right next to the cemetery. When the hedge is trimmed, you can see it from our back lanai. It's huge. Gravestones as far as the eye can—"

"Oh, never mind. Angus, this is it. Number twenty-five. We're here."

Chapter Seventeen

A FEW SECONDS later came the knock on the door.

"I'll get it," Emma said. "Don't worry, I'll take care of everything."

"Thank you. Thank you so much. I owe you." I stood slowly, carefully keeping the baby in position. She clamped down so hard that I was convinced if I let go of her, she'd still be latched on like a circus acrobat.

"Please tell them I'll be right out," I said. "You're sure you can handle it?"

"You leave it to me, Molly."

I sank into the big glider chair in the master bedroom. It would be a while before the baby went to sleep. She was wide awake and hungry. Through the bedroom door I heard Emma let Stephen's parents in. I couldn't make out any words, just the rumble of conversation. Emma's tone and inflection seemed perfectly normal. You wouldn't know she'd been drinking straight gin for the last hour. I don't know how she does it. If it were me, I'd be dragging myself around on my elbows by now.

Finally, Francesca drifted off to sleep. I detached her, placed her in her crib, checked the mirror to make sure everything was dry and in its proper place, and went out to face the music. At least Emma would have filled them in by now. I wouldn't have to break the news about my getting married and having a baby.

Emma, Tiffany, and Angus were sitting around the coffee table in the living room. Emma had not only made coffee, she had placed all three mugs on coasters and set out a bowl of almonds.

"The university's poormouthing," Stephen's mother was telling Emma. "They're giving us this big story about how they get less money from the state every year and they're not allowed to raise their tuition. They're trying to make us think they don't have any money to pay...Molly!"

Stephen's parents looked younger than I remembered them. Angus's hair had thickened and blackened with time, and Tiffany had a lovely new nose, long and slender to fit her face. Her former nose had been a sweet-sixteen gift from her parents. It had had the sharp-tipped, ski-jump shape that now looked dated.

Stephen's parents stood to greet me. We took turns hugging Los Angeles-style, with air kisses instead of actual lip-to-cheek contact. Emma stayed seated and sipped her coffee.

"Tiffany," I said, "you look beautiful." I knew she'd be pleased that I'd noticed her remodeled nose. Stephen's parents were proud of the work their clinic did, and always eager to show it off.

"It's the new nose. I'm glad you like it, Molly. You have such good taste. Well of course you do, that's why you picked our Stephen, right Angus? You know, some people call this an aquiline nose, but that's wrong. I notice you didn't make that mistake."

"Aye," Angus agreed. "Aquiline means ye've a conk like an eagle, wi'a wee bend in it."

Angus's hair wasn't the only thing that had gotten thicker over the years. And why not? Americans adore a Scottish accent. The clients of Park Beverly Hills Cosmetic Center were surely no exception.

"There's no one shape that's right for everyone," Tiffany said.

"So true," I agreed.

I wasn't sure where to take the conversation from there, but a wail from the bedroom decided it for me.

"What on earth was *that*?" Tiffany exclaimed. "It sounds like a baby crying."

I widened my eyes at Emma. She grimaced and shrugged. With all of her chatting and coffee-pouring and almond-setting-out, my whole married-with-a-baby situation apparently hadn't come up.

"Emma," I said, "would you mind bringing everyone up to date? I'll be right back."

I turned and hurried down the hallway before Emma had a chance to wiggle out of it.

When I came back out to the living room, the mood had changed. Stephen's parents looked stricken. Emma had done her job and delivered the news. This was my problem now.

"Molly." Tiffany's voice was uncharacteristically quiet. "You're *married*?"

"I told the lad, didn't I, tae fish or cut bait," Angus said. "It's nae Molly's fault, Tiff."

I held the baby tight to me and shook my head. *No, it most certainly is not my fault.*

"At her age, she canna wait forever," Angus added.

"But Stephen wanted children," Tiffany objected.

"Yeah. He wanted to *date* them," Emma muttered.

I frowned and shook my head at Emma. Fortunately, Stephen's parents hadn't heard her.

Stephen's mother marched up to me,

grasped my shoulders, and looked me and the baby up and down.

"No one told us you were a *mother*, Molly. Why didn't anyone tell us?"

Francesca cooed and batted her chubby arms at Stephen's mother. *Don't rub it in*, I wanted to tell the baby.

"I don't know. I guess Stephen...hm." I was going to say, *I guess Stephen didn't keep you up to date*. But that would sound like I was blaming their dead son.

I guess Stephen has been too busy to tell you about it? No, that would be worse. It would sound like I was still blaming Stephen for not telling them, only being sarcastic about it.

Maybe he did, and you just forgot.

Nope, that wouldn't work. I gave Stephen's mother a shrug and a weak smile.

Tiffany released me and sat back down.

"Angus and I have always appreciated what you did for Stephen," she said. "Nothing changes that."

"Aye," Stephen's father agreed.

"Thank you." I sank into the closest armchair.

Come to think of it, I *had* done a lot for Stephen. Organized his portfolio for him when he went up for promotion. Packed him off to rehab and arranged a cover story for him at work when his addiction got out of control. Refrained from murdering him when I found out why he'd stood me up on my birthday.

"Well," I said, "would anyone like more coffee?"

"Oh yeah," Emma took the cue. "Coffee? Or tea? Molly has tea somewhere, you have tea, right, Molly? Where do you keep your tea?"

Stephen's parents weren't so easily distracted.

"Look at you, Molly. *Married*. And a *baby*." Tiffany had taken on the hearty tone of the runner-up who is trying hard to be a good sport. "So. Are we going to meet the man who stole you away from our Stephen? He must really be something."

And right on cue, we heard the side door open. Donnie came in through the kitchen. He wore the same work uniform as his employees, a red polo shirt with the Drive-

Inn logo. I don't want to be vulgar, so let's just say that Donnie is in excellent physical condition and his shirt was on the close-fitting side.

"Eh, Donnie!" Emma lifted her mug in a sort of greeting.

"Wow," Stephen's mother blurted out. "Is that him?"

"You're home early," I added, unnecessarily.

Chapter Eighteen

I MADE quick introductions as Donnie took the baby from me. Donnie expressed his condolences to Stephen's parents and dispensed handshakes and hugs as appropriate.

"Donnie, what a pleasant surprise," I said. "This is so nice that you could come by."

"It was a little slow at the Drive-Inn, so I thought I'd stop in and see how everyone was doing," he explained.

It was only later that he confessed to me he'd been concerned by how much Emma had been drinking. He'd come back to make sure the baby was safe, and no one was passed out on the floor.

"Will you be joining us for an early dinner, Donnie?" Stephen's mother asked hopefully. This was the first I'd heard of anyone going to dinner.

"Tiffany, I'm sure the man's busy," Angus said.

"I have to get back," Donnie said. "You go, have fun. I'll take Francesca."

Donnie hoisted the baby onto his shoulder, grabbed the diaper bag, and left. Emma made her excuses and followed him out. It was just as well, as it turns out.

The Parks' attorney was waiting for us at the Lehua Inn Coffee Shop. He was conspicuously drab among the colorful tourists, and probably the only person in the hotel who was wearing a suit.

I slid into the vinyl booth next to the man and introduced myself. He told me his name and handed me his card. *If I run into this guy in the street tomorrow,* I thought, *I probably won't recognize him.* His forgettable-ness was certainly deliberate; he probably had many clients like

Stephen's parents, who would not tolerate being upstaged.

"Shall we get started?" he asked. He had a fresh yellow legal pad next to his plate, blank except for the date written at the top of the page. The handwriting was like the man himself, small and spidery.

"Let's get something to eat first," Stephen's mother said. "I'm starving."

I realized I was hungry too. The Lehua Inn's pancake and coffee aroma was tantalizing.

The Lehua Inn's coffee is mediocre and always smells better than it tastes. (Like sin, as the saying goes.) But their pancakes are divine. Give me a stack of golden, hubcap-sized pancakes topped with a foamy ball of butter, bring out a warm, sticky pitcher of maple-flavored syrup to glug over the whole mess, and I can endure anything.

Even a conversation with the parents of my dead ex about suing my employer.

The lawyer took down my name and contact information and asked me to tell him what I could recall.

"From the time you entered the old

Mahina Memorial building," he said. "Please include anything you may have noticed about the condition of the building."

I told him what I could, uncomfortably aware of Stephen's parents sitting across from me. I was telling a story whose grim ending they already knew.

"Why did you exit the building after you visited the washroom?" the lawyer asked.

"I had tried to wash a stain off my blouse. I wanted to give it a chance to dry off a little before I went back to join the others."

No one at the table needed to know about my makeshift paper-towel breast pads. I'd sure learned my lesson that night, though. I now had four pairs of proper pads stuffed in my purse.

"Anyway, when I went outside the door locked behind me," I went on. "So, at that point I had to go around the building. I didn't have a choice. Oh, I did notice that the stairs felt pretty rickety. It might have been termite damage, or rot."

The attorney nodded and made a note.

"How was the lighting?" he asked. "Could you see where you were going?"

"There was no lighting. I don't remember whether the moon was out or anything. Whatever it was doing it was covered up with clouds. That's not unusual for Mahina, though. I had to use the light from my phone to find my way."

He kept writing as I spoke. Then he underlined something.

"And it seems you are...married?" He looked at Tiffany for confirmation. She pursed her lips and nodded.

"But you attended this dinner with Stephen Park."

I stared at him.

"No. I went with Donnie. My husband. We just all ended up at the same table. It was assigned seating. We didn't know in advance who else was going to be at our table."

"What is your husband's full name?"

"Donald Muraco Gonsalves."

"Unusual middle name," the lawyer said.

"It was the name of a famous local wrestler." I spelled the name for him. "His sister's middle name is Bysentenyl. Like two hundred years, except spelled in a unique way. Their parents apparently liked unusual…I guess it's not important. Sorry."

"So at dinner, it was just you and Stephen and your husband?"

"And Bee Corcoran. There were supposed to be two other people sitting with us, but there was a scheduling mix-up and they couldn't make it."

The waitress came by and doled out our giant plates of food. I said grace, crossed myself, and dug in. As soon as my mouth was full of pancake, the attorney cleared his throat.

"Now, I want to ask you about access to the terrace outside. How difficult would it have been, in your view, for someone to gain access to the outdoor terrace?"

He'd caught me off-guard with my cheeks full of pancake. I took a quick gulp of coffee. It didn't have much flavor, which was good, because the flavor it did have was kind of nasty.

"I don't know whether they wanted people going out there," I said. "But there wasn't anything stopping them. There were these tall French doors at the far end of the dining room. I don't remember seeing any velvet ropes or signs that said 'stay off the terrace' or anything like that."

"Were the doors locked?"

"I don't think so. They must have been unlocked for Stephen to get out. So I guess my answer is that it was probably pretty easy to gain access to the terrace."

More writing. Lots of underlining.

"So, a reasonable person would have concluded that it was acceptable to exit the dining room and go out onto the terrace?"

"Probably. Sure."

I was doing exactly what Stephen's parents wanted: putting the university at fault. And the university was at fault. They owned the building, they had decided to open it for an event while they were still doing renovations, they had set up the dinner, and they had left the terrace accessible to guests.

I wasn't sure how to feel about it. On the one hand, I sympathized with Stephen's parents. I couldn't begin to imagine what they were going through. And the university should not have let people wander out onto an unlit terrace with a potentially fatal drop.

On the other hand, Stephen's parents had plenty of money. And the university, my employer, didn't. Except for that big student success grant. Which had so many restrictions on it that it was no help at all.

"When Stephen left your table to go outside, did he go alone?"

"Yes."

"Was there a particular reason he left?"

In fact, he'd turned green and bolted the minute the topic of breastfeeding came up. I decided it wasn't necessary to share that particular detail. It would have disappointed his parents, I think.

"He said he was going outside for a smoke."

"He told us he'd quit," Stephen's mother objected.

"Was anyone else out on the terrace?" the lawyer asked.

"No. At least, not that I saw."

"After Stephen left the table to go

outside for a smoke, when did you see him next?"

Oof. Who thought it would be a good idea to discuss this over dinner?

"When I went outside I saw Stephen up on the terrace, smoking."

"You said it was dark outside," the lawyer said. "You're certain it was Stephen you saw?"

"I recognized the smell," I said. "He smokes those clove cigarettes. Then when I looked up, I saw the glow of the cigarette. Then I heard him calling my name. No, wait, first I heard him say, 'Molly' and that must have been why I looked up…I'm sorry. I'm getting mixed up about the exact order of things."

"You say he called you by name?"

"Yes."

"Did you recognize his voice at that time?"

"Yes."

"And when he called out to you, what did you do?"

I stared at my plate to avoid looking at Stephen's parents.

"Nothing. I kept walking."

"You heard Stephen call out to you, you looked up, and you kept walking?"

"Yes," I said to my pancakes.

"Did you say anything to him?"

I shook my head. *Nothing he could have heard, anyway.*

"Now, I'm sorry to have to ask this," the lawyer said to Stephen's parents. "Did you see him fall? Please think carefully."

"I didn't. I didn't see anything until I turned around. And then he…and then I called for help. And then things happened quickly. Police, and ambulances, and I guess someone must have told the people inside. Bee came running out, but it was too late. She wasn't allowed to touch his body—she wasn't allowed to go near him."

"Who is this Bee person?" Stephen's mother asked.

"Beatrice Corcoran," I said, glad to be the bearer of good news for once. "One of our rising stars. She just won a systemwide research award. She's very impressive." She had also told me that she had no romantic interest in Stephen, but his parents didn't need to know that.

"What does she do?" Tiffany asked.

"She's an assistant professor of kinesiology."

Stephen's mother turned to her husband.

"That's just great. Our son was dating a P.E. teacher."

Stephen's father decided this would be a good time to go pay the bill, and Stephen's mother went to freshen up. This left me sitting next to their attorney.

I cleared my throat. "May I ask you something?"

The attorney paused his writing and looked up, which I took as a "yes."

"What exactly killed him? Stephen?"

The lawyer looked at me like he wasn't sure he'd heard me right.

"He fell from a height of ten meters onto a hard surface," he said slowly.

"No, I know that. But I mean, if he hit his head first, it would've been over quickly. But if it was internal injuries...you know what I'm saying? Stephen didn't suffer, did he? I guess that's what I'm asking."

The furrows on the man's forehead cleared.

"Oh, I see. I don't have that information. We'll know more when the autopsy's done."

It hit me then that Stephen Park was really gone. It must have been the word "autopsy" that got me. I was suddenly desperate to escape the crowded coffee shop with its cloying pancake smell. Stephen's parents were making their way back to the table. As they approached I made a show of glancing at my wrist. Only to remember I wasn't wearing a watch.

"Thank you so much for dinner." I stood and sidled out of the booth. "It was wonderful to see both of you again, very nice to meet you Mister...well. I should be getting back."

"Are ye gonna walk?" Stephen's father asked, surprised. Right. Stephen's parents had driven me over to the hotel.

"I have a ride," I improvised, and before anyone could stop me, I rushed out to the lobby and called Emma.

Chapter Nineteen

IT DIDN'T TAKE LONG for Emma's Prius to zoom up to the front of the Lehua Inn. She was of course dying to know everything that had happened at dinner.

"How about we get down to the Maritime Club before happy hour ends, and you can tell me everything." Emma screeched out of the parking lot and made a two-wheels-off-the-ground left turn onto Hotel Drive.

"Sounds fun, but Donnie has the baby with him at work," I said. "I should probably go pick her up."

"They'll be okay," Emma declared with the confidence of an expert. Which she most definitely is not when it comes to babies.

"I'd feel better going back and relieving Donnie," I said. "I'm not sure a fast-food restaurant is the best place for a baby, and he's not off work for a couple more hours at least. Besides, happy hour at the Maritime Club? What has your poor liver ever done to you?"

"I am very nice to my liver," Emma said.

"Didn't you just drink up all our gin?"

"It wore off already. So fine, no Maritime Club today. Tell me what happened at dinner."

I told Emma everything I could remember.

"I used to get so frustrated with how Stephen's parents would enable him," I said.

"They did enable him," Emma agreed. "Remember that thousand dollar a night rehab or whatever it was? You know it wasn't his theater professor salary paying for it."

"But now that I have Francesca, I understand why they did what they did. He was their child, and he—"

"Nah, you were right the first time," Emma said.

"Okay, maybe he was spoiled. But I didn't realize one of the things about having a baby is, it never stops. By the time your baby's approaching middle age and has tenure, Stephen's parents should've been able to stop worrying about him. But no, you never can stop worrying. Having a kid is a life sentence."

"You should stitch that onto a throw pillow," Emma said. "Having a kid is a life sentence. Anyway, you enabled him too, you know,"

"I know. Thanks for giving me something else to feel bad about."

"Don't feel bad Molly. Stephen's dead."

"How is that supposed to help?"

Emma pulled into the Drive-Inn's lot, and I hopped out to look for Donnie. I found him inside, among the sizzling griddles and bubbling pots that made me so nervous. Francesca wasn't there with him.

"Where's the baby?" Emma asked when I returned to the car empty-handed.

"At the house with Margaret." I pulled

the door shut and buckled in. "He could've let me know before we came all the way here. I walked in and there he was, empty-handed, no baby. I practically had a heart attack."

"How was he supposed to let you know?" Emma pulled out and made a daring left turn into traffic in front of a truck lifted so high the driver probably didn't even see us.

"Emma?" I said. "We just missed getting run over by that truck."

"Nah. We woulda gone right under him. Anyway, don't blame Donnie. You know what it's like when the restaurant's busy. He was running around with his head cut off the whole time, it was probably hard enough for him to get ahold of Margaret."

"Emma, the expression is running around like a *chicken* with its head cut off."

"You know what I mean."

"But now I have the image in my mind of Donnie running around with his head cut off. It's very upsetting. And I've already had an excruciating day."

"See, Molly?"

"See what?"

"You shoulda drank some gin when you had the chance."

I came home to find Margaret at the dining room table. She was balancing Francesca on her lap and reading to her from her CPA review book. I came over to take the baby. Francesca lit up when she saw me. Then she smacked me in the face with her damp little fist and pawed at my blouse.

"I'll get you a glass of water." Margaret jumped up and headed to the kitchen as I got settled on the couch.

"Thank you, Margaret!" I called after her. "And thank you for being available on such short notice."

"I heard you had dinner with Professor Park's parents." She set a tall glass of ice water in front of me. I picked it up and drank most of it before I answered her.

"Well, that news traveled fast. Yes, I did."

"Do you mind if I fix myself a hot chocolate?"

"No, of course not. Help yourself."

Margaret was one of those thin women who always feels cold. I envied her that. I'd love to be able to wear a stylish sweater or jacket now and then without risking heatstroke.

Margaret returned with a mug of hot chocolate, and a second glass of ice water for me. She sat on the couch and hunched over, her slim hands clutching the mug for warmth.

"So…" she asked timidly. "How was it?"

"Seeing Stephen's parents? They're devastated, as you can imagine." I touched Francesca's pulsing cheek. She drew her eyebrows together and ramped up the suction. She apparently didn't appreciate being bothered while she was eating. Fair enough, neither did I.

"It's really nice that you still get along with them even though you aren't seeing Professor Park anymore."

"They're suing Mahina State."

I didn't see any reason to hide the news from Margaret. She was obviously connected to the coconut wireless. She'd hear about it before long anyway.

"Why are they suing the university? What did Mahina State do?"

"It's what we didn't do. We didn't block

off the terrace, we didn't put up lighting, and the railing height wasn't up to modern code. Apparently, it was only twenty-four inches high. Oh, would you mind getting the tape measure from the drawer next to the fridge? I'm curious now."

Margaret disappeared and came back with the tape measure. She measured out twenty-four inches and touched the end of the tape measure to the floor.

"It's low," she said. "Just above my knees."

"Stephen's a little taller than you. And men are more top-heavy because they carry their weight in their shoulders, not their hips. I can see how he would have fallen over."

"So, it was an accident?" Margaret asked brightly.

"Of course it was," I assured her.

Margaret stared into her hot chocolate.

"Why?" I persisted.

"Professor Park was seeing a friend of mine before he started going out with Dr. Corcoran."

"Stephen was seeing a friend of yours?"

Margaret nodded.

"Your age?"

"Yes."

"Ah. Disappointed but not surprised. Have you talked to her since this happened?"

"No. We haven't been in touch." Margaret blew over the top of her mug.

"Why not reach out to her?"

"I don't think she really wants to hear from me. The thing is, I told her it was a bad idea to get involved with Professor Park. I mean, if I were about to make a big mistake, I'd want someone to try to stop me. That's the only reason I said anything. But I guess she didn't feel the same way."

"You didn't approve of her getting involved with Stephen?" I asked.

"It wasn't just getting involved with him. She turned down a full-ride scholarship to a graduate program in actuarial science. Just to stay in Mahina to be with him."

"She turned down a full ride?"

Margaret nodded vigorously. I could tell she was still upset about her friend's decision. I didn't blame her. I didn't even know this young woman, and now I felt the urge to go shake some sense into her.

"Professor, do you think I should tell Professor Park's parents?"

"That Stephen had been seeing your friend?"

She nodded.

"I don't know. What would it accomplish now? Would it make them feel any better?"

"They would know that somebody loved their son," she said "Sorry, I mean, you must have too, of course, but…I don't know."

"I'm not sure they're ready to deal with anything else at this point. If you don't mind my asking, who is this 'friend' you're referring to?"

I couldn't imagine that Margaret herself been one of Stephen's conquests. She seemed far too sensible to fall for him. But then again, so did I.

"Her name is Verna Jackson-Brown," Margaret said.

"Her last name is really Jackson Browne?" I asked.

"Yes. Why?" Margaret asked.

"Like the singer?"

Margaret shook her head

"Who?" she asked, which made me feel very old.

"Wait a minute." I rested my hand on Francesca's fuzzy head. "Verna Jackson-Brown? Isn't Verna the name of Betty and Niall's daughter? Betty Jackson, in psychology. Is that your friend's mom?"

"Verna's mom is a psych professor," Margaret said brightly. "Yes, I think that's right."

"Stephen Park was dating Betty Jackson's *daughter?*"

Margaret shrugged. "I guess so?"

"Does Betty Jackson know?"

"No, I don't think so. She said they'd kick her out if they knew. Um, can I get more chocolate, Professor? It's really good."

"Of course. Help yourself. And please call me Molly. You're not my student anymore. Unless you're more comfortable calling me Professor...I don't know, do whatever you want. But if you're going into the kitchen, can you refill my water glass?"

"Were those really Professor Park's

parents you had dinner with?" She called back from the kitchen.

"Yes, why?"

"My friend who works at the Lehua Inn told me they were both haole."

"They are."

"But Stephen is Korean. Is he adopted?"

She came back with two glasses of water for me. I picked up one and drank half of it in a single gulp.

"Thank you," I said, "That's perfect. I can't believe this is coming up again. Who told you Stephen Park was Korean?"

"Verna. She said she and Stephen had that in common, their mixed background."

I suppressed a snort.

"Park is a Korean name," Margaret added, a little defensively. "Isn't it?"

I touched Francesca's little nose. "Well Stephen Park is just a big poser, isn't he?" I cooed. "Park is a Scots name. Stephen let people assume he was half-Korean because in his mind it's cooler to be half-Korean than just a plain old white guy."

Margaret looked puzzled.

"So he's not hapa? I mean, he wasn't?"

"He was Scottish and Jewish, if you want to call that hapa, but he was not even remotely Korean. He just liked to let people think he was."

"What? I don't understand. Why?"

"I guess in his mind being Korean was trendy or something. I don't know."

"But didn't that hurt his parents' feelings?" Margaret asked.

"I don't think they knew. And I'm sure not going to be the one to tell them."

Chapter Twenty

IT WASN'T until Donnie came home that night that something clicked into place in my memory. I sat at the counter holding the baby, while he was busy trying to fit foil trays of leftovers into our refrigerator. Donnie lets the staff take home extra food at the end of the day, and whatever they leave, we get.

"Donnie, do you remember Betty Jackson, who I waved to last night?"

Donnie wrote *Chicken Chow Fun* on a length of blue masking tape and pressed it onto the end of the foil tray.

"Betty? Yes. Your friend, the psychology

professor. Her husband's name is Niall Brown. And they have…four kids?"

"Wow, good memory! *Five* kids, though. The oldest is named Verna. I just found out she's already graduated from college. Donnie, I think she was the one who waited on us at the donor dinner."

"Who?" Donnie asked from inside the refrigerator.

"Betty Jackson's daughter. Verna Jackson-Brown. Remember, pretty girl, tall, green eyes? She poured the wine? Maybe you were away from the table. Donnie, what would you do if one of baby Francesca's professors tried to date her? When she's in college, I mean. She obviously doesn't have any professors now, because she's a baby."

Donnie stood up and looked at me over the refrigerator door.

"I'd kill him," he said evenly, and went back to fridge-arranging.

"Not literally, though," I said. "You mean you wouldn't be happy about it. You're exaggerating for effect, right?"

"Maybe," he replied.

"Yeah, I know what you mean." I

watched the baby sleeping in my arms, her little chest rising and falling evenly. If someone ever tried to harm Francesca, or take advantage of her the way Stephen Park took advantage of his students, I would destroy him.

I wondered whether that might not be very Christian of me. I made a mental note to mention it the next time I happened to go to Confession.

Donnie finished fitting everything into the fridge, poured two glasses of Sangiovese, and came over to sit with Francesca and me.

"Why are you talking about Francesca's professors trying to date her?" Donnie reached over and gently stroked the baby's fuzzy black hair. "It would be terrible. I don't even want to think about it."

"Me neither. But Verna, Betty and Niall's daughter? The one who was serving us? Apparently, she was dating Stephen Park."

Donnie shook his head.

"Do the parents know?"

"I don't know."

Donnie raised his eyebrows.

"Were you thinking your friend Betty Jackson might have had something to do with Stephen Park's death?"

"What? I wasn't even thinking of that," I lied.

"When you asked me how I'd react, isn't that what you had in mind?"

"I don't know. I know I'm not a detective, it's not really any of my business who killed whom, but the thing is I know everyone involved in this, so it's kind of hard not to think about it. But Donnie, just follow me here. Betty Jackson is sitting at her table at the far end of the dining hall, right?"

"I remember she waved to you."

"Exactly. So she's over there, she sees Stephen is at a table across the dining room, her daughter Verna is working for the catering company waiting tables, Betty watches her daughter interacting with Stephen—"

"Interacting in what way?" Donnie asked.

"The daughter came around to refill drinks. I don't know, it seemed there was some kind of weird eye contact. Or non-contact, because they wouldn't look at each other. Anyway. Betty knows Stephen is there. She waits for him to go out for a smoke and follows him onto the terrace, and then…what? Waits until he's distracted by the sight of someone walking by underneath? And sneaks up, shoves him over the edge, and runs back inside?"

"That 'someone' walking by being you?" Donnie asked.

"Yes. It's been bothering me, to be honest. Donnie, if I hadn't been walking by at that exact moment—"

"Molly, it wasn't your fault."

"Thank you for saying that. I've been thinking about it a lot. If I hadn't walked by right then, Stephen might still be alive."

"Maybe not," Donnie said thoughtfully.

"If Betty Jackson were planning on killing someone," I said, "which seems highly unlikely, but let's just say she wanted to protect her daughter, which I can understand. Betty would have a much better plan than just running out and shoving Stephen over the railing. Think of how many ways it could've gone wrong. What if Stephen had called for help, or shouted, *Hey, Betty Jackson from the psychology department, why are you pushing me to my death?*"

"Are you sure it was Stephen's voice you heard calling you?" Donnie asked.

"I don't know. At the time I was sure it was Stephen. Who else could it have been?"

"Someone who killed Stephen Park and wanted you to think he was still alive?"

"Ew, that's grotesque. Someone imitates him and then drops his dead body onto the ground?"

"Sorry, I'm not as good as you and Emma at thinking about murders."

"No, you're quite good at it. Disturbingly good. Donnie, should I tell Betty? About her daughter and Stephen?"

Donnie glanced at the baby.

"I think a few months ago if you'd asked me, I would've said to stay out of it. But now, I'd want to know if it were Francesca."

Chapter Twenty-One

THE IDEA of happy hour at the Maritime Club had been growing on me ever since Emma suggested it. We used to go all the time before the baby came. So the next afternoon I arranged to meet Emma there. It would be just like old times, I thought.

The Maritime Club was exactly as I remembered it. Weather-beaten clubhouse, an unparalleled view of the blue ocean, and waves crashing on the rocks so close that we got misted with salty seawater. Emma had bought a membership because she thought her husband Yoshi might like it. Yoshi had just moved to Mahina and made no secret of how unimpressed he was. He would say things like, "an Ivy League MBA doesn't belong in a place like this." Yoshi's mellowed a lot since then. He gave up on finding a "suitable" job, took up canoe paddling, and now spends most of his time at the bayfront. These days he thinks the Maritime Club is too pretentious.

The Maritime Club's menu probably hadn't changed since Hawaii became a state. Today's complimentary happy hour snack was rumaki and greasy egg rolls, served with a red-and-yellow yin-yang of ketchup and mustard. To avoid disturbing the other diners we sat outside on the lanai, where the sound of the waves crashing on the rocks would compete with any baby noise. Francesca kept trying to wiggle out of my arms and onto the floor (which was not going to happen). She fussed when I thwarted her, and she also needed a few diaper changes and feedings, but overall, she was an exemplary baby.

"Well, that was an experience," Emma said as she signed the check.

"It was nice to get out," I said. "We should do this again."

"Yeah. Maybe fifteen or twenty years from now."

"Don't you worry about Auntie Emma," I cooed as I wrestled Francesca's car seat into the base. The Thunderbird's soft top didn't leave me much room to maneuver, but I had to keep the top up if I didn't want the baby getting rained on. "It's been a long time since she was a baby. She doesn't remember what it was like. When you're being held, you want to go explore. When you're out exploring, you want someone to hold you. I understand."

"Beh," Francesca replied.

I had just gotten buckled in and was about to turn the key when a diaper blast shook the car. Then, like thunder follows lightning, came the smell. I unbuckled myself, unbuckled the baby, grabbed the diaper bag, and went back inside to change her in the bathroom. By the time we got on the road, I was feeling fairly frazzled.

When we arrived at home I was surprised to see Donnie's car in the garage. I felt the hood. It was cool. He'd been here for a while. Very odd.

We came in to find Donnie on the living room couch, glass of whiskey in his hand. The bottle was on the coffee table. He looked shell-shocked.

"Donnie?"

It seemed like he didn't even hear me. I put the sleeping baby in her crib, turned on the baby monitor, and came back out to the living room.

"Molly," he said, as if he had just noticed I was there.

I sat down next to him, gently took the whiskey glass from his hand, and sipped it.

"That's the one you don't like," he said as I started coughing.

"Donnie. You're home early, you look like someone pithed you, and you're drinking this stuff that tastes like a tire fire. What is going on?"

"It's peated."

"What?"

"They burn peat to dry the barley. That gives it the smoky flavor."

"Donnie."

He turned to look at me, finally.

"I was arrested," he said.

"What? Why? For what?"

Donnie took the tire-fire whiskey back and downed it in one gulp.

"For killing Stephen Park."

"They arrested you? They didn't drag you out of the restaurant, did they?"

Donnie shook his head.

"Medeiros called and told me to come down to the station."

"So he literally phoned it in."

"It was a courtesy."

"So did you go?"

Donnie nodded.

"But you're here. I guess they figure you're not a flight risk. They released you on your own recognizance?" I was proud of myself for remembering the correct legal term.

"It wasn't quite that easy. Bail was fifty thousand."

"Fifty thousand *dollars*? Donnie, where on earth—"

"The home equity line of credit."

"That we were going to use for Francesca's college? Oh, listen. She knows we're talking about her."

Francesca's gentle fussing crackled through the baby monitor. I went back to get her.

"Here. Say hi to your daughter. She missed you."

I plopped the baby into Donnie's arms and went to pour myself a glass of wine. Thus equipped, I returned to the living room and sat next to my husband and daughter.

"Do you think it's okay having all this alcohol around the baby?" I asked.

"She's not drinking it."

"Fair enough." I clicked my glass against his.

"Where did you go this afternoon?" Donnie asked. "I thought you'd be here."

"We went to the Maritime Club for happy hour."

"With the baby?"

"Yeah. Emma and I hadn't been in a while. It wasn't as relaxing as I remember it. Donnie, what is going on? Why, and how, were you supposed to have killed Stephen Park? I was there with you at the donor dinner. I can vouch for you."

"No, you can't, Molly." Donnie stroked the baby's head.

"Well, okay, maybe they won't take my word for it because I'm your wife. But Donnie, you were nowhere near Stephen when he fell. You only left the table the one time to take Margaret's phone call."

Donnie shook his head.

"Okay, maybe I left the table two times. But Bee Corcoran was there. She should be able to tell them where you were that night. Anyway, what's your motive supposed to be?"

Donnie frowned a little.

"You," he said.

"What?"

"That's their thinking."

"Me? You mean because I briefly dated Stephen, like a hundred years ago when I first came to Hawaii, before I even met you?"

Donnie nodded.

"Well, that's an idiotic theory, and it doesn't make any sense. Unless you believe that your wife is like a pair of shoes that you don't want anyone else trying on before you buy them. Even then, you don't go track down the person who tried on your shoes and kill them. You just disinfect your shoes…never mind. I'm not sure where I was going with that. Donnie, my point is that we'll just have to find one of the servers or someone at another table who can attest that you didn't go anywhere." I stood up. "Look, you've just been through a lot. Maybe you should get something on your stomach. Have you eaten? I'll go warm up some Korean chicken."

"Go ahead and get some for yourself. I'm not hungry. We'll be right here. The baby and me."

I sat back down.

"Donnie, is there something you're not telling me?"

Chapter Twenty-Two

I SAT in the dark living room, nursing the baby. Donnie had finally gone to bed, but I couldn't sleep. (This was fine with the baby, who was awake and hungry.)

I had assumed that Donnie had been nowhere near Stephen that night.

According to Donnie, I was wrong.

Donnie told me he had been bothered by Stephen's waspish comments, but felt he couldn't say anything because he didn't want to make a scene. When I left the table for the second time, only Donnie and Bee remained; Stephen had already gone out for a smoke. Then someone Bee knew came over to chat with her. No longer obliged to make conversation with Bee, Donnie had gone outside to confront Stephen.

"But as soon as I stepped out there I said to myself, this is crazy," Donnie told me. "I went back inside right away."

"Did you see Stephen out there?" I asked.

"I didn't see anything. It was dark."

I told myself I believed Donnie. I accepted his story the way I accept that radio waves can travel through empty space. Even though I can't get my mind around the idea that a wave motion can travel through a vacuum when there's nothing there to move.

But at the same time, I could understand why the police might not have been so credulous.

Stephen had been especially unpleasant that evening. There was his usual snide banter about my being a bourgeois business-school sellout, but that had been going on for years. It had started back when *The County Courier* was still doing actual reporting, and they'd published the salaries of Mahina State's employees. Stephen discovered I out-earned him, and never forgave me for it. Like it was my fault the business school paid better than the theater department.

Then there was the needling about my being complicit in The Patriarchy by getting married and having a baby. After Stephen ditched me for his teenage student I guess he expected me to sit around lighting candles in front of his picture or something. Instead I moved on and married Donnie. Which was also unforgiveable in his book.

But something had been different this time. Stephen hadn't blunted his poison barbs with his characteristic "just kidding" smirk. He scowled the whole time, as if it literally pained him to share a table with me. A few times he even rubbed the back of his neck (we get it, Stephen. Having to sit with us is a pain in the neck, so clever).

I didn't blame Donnie for wanting to have a word with Stephen. I could have pushed him over that railing myself. Not that I would share these thoughts with Detective Medeiros.

My phone jangled, startling the baby in

the middle of her meal (ouch). I answered it as quickly as I could.

It was my mother. A woman with years of top-notch medical training and experience, who still didn't get the concept of time zones.

"Mom. Is everything okay? It's so early."

"It's seven-thirty, Molly. How late do you usually sleep?"

"It's four-thirty in Hawaii."

"AM or PM?"

"AM. If it were four-thirty in the afternoon, I wouldn't have said it was early."

"Well, you sound alert. It seems I didn't wake you up." This was as close to an apology as I would get.

"No, but the ringing phone scared the baby. Don't worry about me. Who needs two nipples?"

"Molly, that Stephen Park's parents called me. What on earth is going on over there?"

"Stephen's parents...right, well there has been some unfortunate news, but I didn't tell you because I didn't want to worry you—"

"They told me Stephen is dead. Is it true?"

"Yes. Sorry."

Why was I apologizing? I didn't kill him.

I tried to predict what I was going to get scolded about next. Either my mother was going to ask why she didn't hear it from me first and make me feel guilty about keeping her in the dark, or she'd take the opportunity to warn me about lurking dangers in my life that I couldn't be trusted to navigate and that were also somehow, vaguely, my fault.

"I must say the news rather caught me flat-footed. Stephen's parents seemed to assume that you had already told me, which of course you didn't."

"Well, this whole thing just happened, and things have been a little hectic—"

"It seems your university does a terrible job of maintaining their buildings. They're very unsafe. Are you sure your building is safe? Remember, you're a mother now, with a helpless little human depending on you. You can't just live for yourself anymore."

So one from column A, one from column B.

"Mom, I didn't tell you because I didn't want you and Dad to worry. Hi Dad."

"Hiya sweet pea. How'd you know I was here?"

"Lucky guess." Whenever my mom calls, my dad is lurking cheerfully in the background. Always.

"How's little Frankie?" he asked.

I looked down at Francesca, who had recovered from the interruption and was once again happily chowing down. Her eyes were closed, but her cheeks were pulsating furiously.

"That's not really her nickname, Dad. We just call her The Baby." I disliked the name Frankie, but I didn't want to hurt his feelings.

"She's right dear," My mother said. "It's not very feminine."

"The Baby just fits her better," I said. "Although I guess it'll only work until we have another one. If you have two babies you can't just call one The Baby."

"Molly, your optimism is wonderful, but

let's stick to reality, shall we? You were just under the wire with this one. It would be madness to try again at your age."

"Thank you for the tactful reminder, Mom. But we could always adopt like you guys did."

"Oh, no, I would never recommend adoption," my mother said. "Not if you have other options. It's like buying a pig in a poke. You have no idea what you're going to get."

"Okay. Thanks, Mom."

"Just do your best for little Fanny. Oh, and send a card or something to Stephen's parents. I don't want them to think we've raised a boor."

"I'm sure that's their main concern right now. Don't worry, I won't forget. And her name isn't Fanny either."

It wasn't long before Donnie was up and getting ready to go to work. He fixed himself a coffee and sat down at the counter. I put the sleeping baby down in her crib and came back out to join him.

"How are you feeling this morning?" I asked.

He pulled me close and kissed my forehead.

"Better. I got in touch with Honey Akiona. I'm thinking of asking her to represent me. If it's okay with you."

"Yes, of course it's okay with me. Why wouldn't it be? You should have a great defense lawyer."

I had known Honey Akiona since before she went off to law school and returned to become one of Mahina's most prominent criminal defense attorneys. She had taken an introductory business class from me years ago. Even back then she had been smart, fearless, and not particularly concerned about coloring inside the lines.

"It's going to cost some money," Donnie said.

"Donnie, what is money for if not to influence the criminal justice system in one's own favor? Besides, you hired Honey to represent me that time I was in a wee spot of trouble. Don't you remember?"

Donnie smiled a little.

"How could I forget? But we weren't married yet. It was just my money then.

Now it's our money. That's right, you *were* in pretty deep—"

"Yes, well, I didn't mean to rehash all that old news right now, but my point is, even though this is a silly misunderstanding, it's best to hire someone who can help us get through it as quickly and painlessly as possible."

"Okay." Donnie gulped the rest of his coffee and stood. "I need to get going. I'll see you two this afternoon. Hopefully there won't be any more surprises between now and then."

Chapter Twenty-Three

BY MIDMORNING the household was back to its usual routine. Margaret was reading accounting rules to Francesca, and I was neck-deep in Student Retention Office paperwork, when the phone rang.

It was Betty Jackson calling.

I wondered whether she knew what Margaret had told me, about her daughter Verna being involved with Stephen Park. Should I tell Betty? I'd want to know if it were my daughter. On the other hand, I didn't want to be the one to deliver the news.

"Molly," Betty said, "I heard about Donnie's arrest. Are you okay?"

"Yes, just a minute."

I took the phone out onto the front porch, where the reception was better. I had long gotten over any worries about my neighbors seeing me in sweat pants and a ratty t-shirt. I felt too jumpy to sit, so I paced.

"Thank you for asking," I said. "I'm doing as well as can be expected when one's husband's been arrested for murdering one's ex-boyfriend."

"Sounds reasonable," she said. "Is this a good time to call? I didn't even ask."

"No, it's nice to be interrupted. I was just trying to figure out how to do a particular data query for one of my Student Retention Office reports."

"Do I want to know?" Betty asked.

"No, but I'll tell you anyway. I'm supposed to show that students have greater success in classes with 'engaged' professors. Regardless of class size, student preparation, or whether the professor is part-time or tenure-track."

"They tell you what conclusion they

want, and you're supposed to find it? Oh lordy."

"They tell me what conclusion the *foundation* wants, and if we find it, we keep our grant funding for another year."

Betty Jackson is a psychometrician. She specializes in measuring things like student success, and is a coauthor of one of the field's most popular textbooks. Her name was even on the original grant application that funded the Student Retention Office. I don't know the whole history, but I do know that nowadays the Student Retention Office won't even let her see their data.

"Just out of morbid curiosity," Betty said. "How are they measuring student success?"

"By the student's final grade in the class."

"And how do you know which professors are 'engaged'?"

"Easy. They're the ones who give out the highest grades."

"Uh huh. And they're going to use your results to...?"

"To show that handing out those tablets with the proprietary software increases faculty engagement and student success."

"I thought the Student Retention Office gave those tablets to everyone."

"They did."

"So there's no comparison group."

"Nope. Because if you had a comparison group, you might find out that your groundbreaking innovation doesn't make a difference. And that would be an unacceptable result."

"Oh, don't I know it. Look on the bright side, Molly. It's not every day you find such a perfect real-life example of 'begging the question.' You still like being department chair?"

"Hate it."

"Okay."

"But if I step down, Rodge Cowper becomes chair and that would be even worse. How did you hear about Donnie's arrest by the way? Was it in the paper already?"

"The online police blotter on *Island Confidential*. Didn't you see it?"

"I guess not."

"Molly, I thought you of all people would have kept up with *Island Confidential*.

You and Pat haven't had a falling out, have you?"

"I guess when the baby came I got out of the habit of reading it. I wanted to avoid bad news. Wow, I haven't talked to Pat Flanagan in ages, come to think of it. Not since the baby was born."

"It happens when you have kids," Betty said. "It's easy to drift away from your friends."

From the back side of the house I heard the revving of a distant lawnmower. They were mowing the graveyard.

"I should call Pat," I said.

"You should, Molly. He's on good terms with Mahina PD and can give you the scoops, so to say, on Donnie's case. But I called for another reason. Do you remember my daughter Verna?"

What would I say when she asked me what I knew about her daughter and Stephen? I wasn't even certain it was true. I'd let Betty tell me, and then I'd try to act surprised.

"Uh, yes. She was one of the servers at the dinner, wasn't she?"

"Yes, she was. Verna is working part-time at a catering company. That quarter-million-dollar liberal-arts degree sure is paying off. Anyway. Since then, she did a dinner event at the Maritime Club. Dean Gunderson, have you met our new Arts & Sciences dean?"

"I talked to him at the dinner," I said. "He seems nice."

"Yes, doesn't he? Well. He happened to be sitting with Ray Pang."

"The prosecutor?"

"M-hm. I will repeat to you what Verna claims she overheard. I do not vouch for its authenticity or truthfulness, and I will deny having told you any of this."

"Disclaimer noted." I tried to sound calm, but I noticed my pacing had picked up speed.

"It seems that Gunderson was lobbying the prosecutor to put Stephen's death down to murder, rather than accident."

I peeked in the window to make sure Margaret wasn't listening in. She wasn't. She was sitting on the couch, reading to Francesca from her CPA exam flashcards.

"Why would they want to do that?" I asked.

"I have my own theory. But I'd like to hear what you think."

I considered it for a moment.

"They want Stephen's death to be a murder. Hmm. Because if they can pin Stephen's death on the jealous husband of his victim's ex, then they're not liable and they don't have to pay anything to the bereaved parents?"

"Bingo," Betty said. "Do you have another call coming in?"

I did.

"Dan Watanabe," I said. "I'll swipe it to voice mail."

"Your dean? You're not on duty over the summer, are you?"

"No. He's probably trying to get me to serve on some committee for free. I'm going to ignore him and let him call the next sucker. I'm already spending too much time on these stupid Student Retention Office reports."

"Good plan."

"Betty, thank you for telling me about

this. What do you think I should do? Should I tell Stephen's parents?"

"Well, that's up to you," Betty said. "I'm just passing it along because I thought you'd want to know. I'm sure you'd do the same for me."

Dang it.

"Um, Betty? I was actually going to call you. To tell you something I'd heard. I have no idea whether it's true or not, but, you know, just like you told me, and I appreciated it..."

"Sure. What is it?"

"It's about Verna."

"Ah. Does it have to do with the late Stephen Park?"

"Kind of. Someone told me they were romantically involved."

"Yes. I knew about that."

"You did?"

"But thank you for telling me."

"Does your daughter know you know?"

"She's never said anything to me. But if I didn't know before, I'd have to ask myself why she was so interested in listening in on a conversation about Stephen Park."

"Well, he did die. I guess that makes it interesting."

"What I don't understand is, why arrest Donnie of all people?" Betty said. "Donnie is the most level-headed person I've ever met. Niall and I have as much of a motive as anyone, Stephen breaking our little girl's heart like he did. And I was there at the dinner. Why didn't anyone arrest me?"

"Donnie admits he followed Stephen out onto the terrace," I said.

"Oh my. That is unfortunate."

That evening, after dinner, I told Donnie what Betty had told me. His arrest was a deliberate act of misdirection, I said. The university just wanted to avoid paying for Stephen's death.

He sat and rocked the baby and nodded as if he were listening, but it seemed like he wasn't really processing it.

"Donnie," I persisted, "I know it's second- or third-hand information, but this is 'Pay-to-play Ray.' The prosecutor who made our chancellor's DUIs magically disappear. It's not like it's out of character for him to go along with something like this. Maybe you want to tell your lawyer about it? That the university is looking for a fall guy so they're not liable?"

Donnie shook his head.

"I can call her myself," I offered. "That might be even better. You might not remember all the details."

"Please, Molly, don't...let's just let her do her job. She's going to be getting in touch with you anyway to take your statement. I'm going to bed."

"Donnie, it's not even eight o'clock."

I took Francesca from him.

"Thanks," he said, without looking at me. He stood up and headed down the hallway to our bedroom.

Chapter Twenty-Four

I DIDN'T TAKE action until the next day. Donnie had left, and Margaret was supervising the baby's tummy time. Francesca was supposed to sleep face-up, but not spend all of her time that way lest she develop a weak back and a flat head. Francesca didn't particularly enjoy tummy time. She struggled to lift her head (which, admittedly, was massive compared to the rest of her). Francesca always seemed relieved when her exercise sessions were over. In this way she was truly her mother's daughter.

I set down my coffee cup and found my purse.

"Margaret?" I said.

"Francesca, look up here at Aunty Margaret. Good job, baby! Sorry, what?"

"I'm going out for a few minutes."

"Oh. Okay. Baby's doing a good job with tummy time, yes she is."

I went to the garage, started up the Thunderbird, and dug around until I found the business card I was looking for.

Ah, here it was. I pulled out the card and called Stephen's parents' attorney. I left a message detailing what Betty had told me: that Geoffrey Gunderson had conspired with the county prosecutor to pin Stephen's death on Donnie. Donnie had told me not to talk to *his* lawyer. He hadn't said don't tell *any* lawyer.

Then I called Emma and caught her up.

"Molly, forget about working this morning," Emma said excitedly. "We gotta brainstorm."

"Margaret's here at the house," I said.

"Can she hear you?"

"No. I'm calling from my car."

"Let's meet somewhere. Not here.

Yoshi's got his t-shirt printing junk everywhere. How about the Pair-O-Dice?"

"The Pair-O-Dice? Is that place still around?" Every time I had gone there, the place had been practically empty. I had no idea how they stayed in business.

"Whaddaya mean is that place still around? Molly, the Pair-O-Dice is like four blocks from your house. How do you not know it's still there?"

"It's three quarters of a mile from my house. And I haven't had a lot of opportunities to go strolling around downtown Mahina lately."

"You're not gonna bring the baby, are you?" Emma asked warily.

"I told you, she's with Margaret."

"Until when?"

"Until this afternoon. Around two, whenever Donnie comes home for lunch. I can be down there in half an hour."

"Never takes half an hour to drive from your place."

"I'm going to walk. I don't want to deal with parallel-parking the Thunderbird downtown. Besides, it's not raining, and I can use the exercise."

I went inside and checked on Margaret and the baby one last time to make sure they were okay. Everything seemed fine. Margaret was sitting in one of our big armchairs, holding Francesca in her lap and reading to her from the CPA exam flash cards.

Donnie's Drive-Inn looked crowded when I passed. The lines at the order windows were three or four deep, and people were standing around waiting for one of the picnic tables to clear. Good. We were going to have to sell a lot of plate lunches to pay for Donnie's lawyer. I continued downhill, past the Victorian post office building. By the time I passed the park and reached the intersection. my surroundings had gone from quaint to charmingly sketchy. Rain-battered old-West style storefronts mingled with disused gas stations, ramshackle plantation houses, and makeshift hostels with hand painted signs.

By the time I reached the Pair-O-Dice Bar & Grille, I was out of "charmingly sketchy" territory and had entered plain old "sketchy." When the Pair-O-Dice's festive neon sign was turned on, the pink dice tumbled, and the green palm trees did a stop-motion sway. But now, in the drizzly midday, the sign was merely a scribble of dusty tubing in a black window. Sun-faded flyers taped behind the glass announced concerts and craft fairs that had taken place months ago.

Once my eyes adjusted to the Pair-O-Dice's dark interior, it took no time at all to locate Emma. She was the only living soul there. She was most of the way through a tall glass of beer.

"Emma, It's not even lunchtime." I took a seat at the wobbly table and popped the tab of the canned club soda Emma had procured for me. She knows I'll only order canned drinks here.

"Not that I'm judging," I added. "Thanks for this.

"The Pair-O-Dice has its own time zone." Emma pointed to the darkened window. "Once we're on this side of that neon sign, it's eternal happy hour. You're okay? Baby's squared away?"

"The baby's fine. When I left, Margaret was reading something to her about par versus book value. I'll have to borrow her note cards for when I have trouble sleeping. Emma, guess what I just found out. Apparently Verna, Betty Jackson's daughter, turned down a grad school scholarship in actuarial science to stay in Mahina with Stephen Park."

Emma tilted her head.

"What does Betty Jackson's daughter have to do with Stephen?"

"Oh, I guess I never got a chance to tell you. Betty's daughter and Stephen Park were a thing."

"Ew!" Emma set down her beer and shook her hands as if they were covered with bugs.

"Didn't I tell you?"

"No!" Emma cried. "I think I would've remembered. Poor Betty."

In any other establishment, Emma's outburst would have turned heads. But there were no heads to turn at the Pair-O-

Dice. Even the bartender was mysteriously AWOL. At least as far as I could tell, although it was dark enough that someone might have been standing behind the bar without my realizing it.

"I didn't tell you? I guess I told Donnie about it," I said.

"Oh, and that's the same as telling me about it? Cause we all look alike to you?"

"Yes, you and Donnie look exactly alike to me. That's the explanation. Actually, I think it's because you're both in my 'close confidant' category."

"Well, tell me then. What's the deal with Park and Betty's daughter?"

I told Emma everything I could think of that she might have missed.

Emma shook her head.

"Man. I don't even have a kid, but I can tell you, if it was my daughter? I'd want to kill him. You sure Betty or Niall didn't shove him off that balcony?"

"No, I'm not sure. Nor would I blame them."

"But they think they can pin it on Donnie," Emma mused. "It's weird. With all the people around who had something against Park, how come they focus on Donnie? He can prove he was inside when Stephen fell."

"Actually, he can't."

"What?"

"He told me he went outside to talk to Stephen."

"He did what?" Emma slammed her beer down on the wooden table. I picked up a napkin and wiped beer foam from my eye.

"He didn't like the way Stephen was talking to me. But he didn't do anything to Stephen. He told me as soon as he was outside he realized he was making a mistake. He changed his mind and came back inside."

"Molly, how come you're keeping all the interesting stuff from me? I thought we were friends."

"And that's why we're here," I reassured her. "To get caught up. I've been replaying that night in my mind. So we were at Table 4—"

"Whoa, table four?"

"You don't have to be sarcastic, Emma."

"I'm not. Four is unlucky. It means death."

"What?"

"In Japanese, four is pronounced *shi*, which sounds like the word for death. That's how come you're not supposed to give gifts that are in sets of four."

"Oh good. Yet another opportunity for me to make a horrible social blunder without realizing—hang on."

I reached for the ringing phone in my bag. Dan Watanabe's office number flashed on my screen.

"Speaking of deans. *Dang* it. What does Dan want now?"

"Don't answer it," Emma urged me. "He's gonna try put you on a committee."

"He's tried calling already," I said. "Maybe it's important."

"And he can't get another sucker, so he's trying you again. Molly, don't. It's a trap."

But I had already pressed the answer button.

Chapter Twenty-Five

DAN WASN'T TRYING to press-gang me onto a summer committee. In fact, he had called to do me a favor. He had negotiated space in the new building for the College of Commerce, he said, and he was going to let me pick out my office.

"The other faculty members are bugging me about it," he said, "but I said I'd let the department chairs have first dibs, and I'm keeping my word."

"Thanks Dan," I said. "I appreciate it."

Across the table from me, Emma turned her head sideways like an owl.

"Well, I appreciate what you guys do too, Molly."

"You mean like work for free during our unpaid summers?"

"Yeah. Like that. Management department has the top floor, by the way," he added.

"The top floor, huh? Because we're the most important?"

Emma rolled her eyes and stood up for another trip to the bar.

"Because you're the smallest department, and there are only four usable offices up there. This way you're all together."

"Only four *usable* offices? What are the unusable offices, where they store their old straitjackets and lobotomy icepicks?"

"I couldn't say. They're not quite done fixing up the building."

"Yeah, that was pretty evident at the donor dinner." I didn't know whether Dan had heard about Stephen Park's death. Serena, his secretary, would tell him if she hadn't already. "Too bad you couldn't be there, by the way. I mean it."

"Yes, I heard what happened, Molly. I wasn't sure whether to tell you I'm sorry for your loss."

So he had heard.

"It's not my loss, particularly, but it's a shame."

"By the way, you mentioned the donor dinner? We're not in that building."

"We're not? We don't get the fabulous entryway with the curving staircases?"

"No, we have the building behind the main hospital."

"There's another building? Where? I didn't see it."

"Directly in back, a little further down the hill. It's kind of overgrown back there. You wouldn't notice it unless you were looking for it. It used to be the nurses' quarters or a leprosy ward or something."

"I wish you had just said nurses' quarters."

Emma came over and sat back down. She had a tall glass of beer in one hand and a miniature wine bottle in the other.

"Seems like you need this." She handed me the wine.

"Is that Emma Nakamura?" Dan asked. "Tell her hi for me. You guys keeping up your coffee breaks this summer?"

Dan knew Emma well. During the school year she made a habit of hanging around my office and mooching coffee from my espresso machine.

"Yes," I said as I unscrewed the top from the wine bottle. "Can't let that coffee break tradition go. So, when should I go pick out my office?"

"Sooner's better than later. I'd go today if I were you. If anything's locked, you can call security to let you in. Make sure you have your ID."

"See?" Emma said, as soon as I hung up. "Told you it was a good idea to answer the phone."

"Uh-huh. Hey, thanks for the wine."

"You're lucky," she said. "Your dean's a decent guy."

"I know."

Emma lifted her glass, clinked it against my little wine bottle, and drank.

"Want another one?" she asked.

"No thank you. I just started this one. Emma, we have some time. Margaret has the baby. Want to come help me pick out my new office?"

"Sure. Might be fun." Emma picked up her glass, realized she'd already emptied it, and set it back down again.

Chapter Twenty-Six

"SO I'VE BEEN THINKING," I said as I climbed into Emma's undersized front seat. "About our theory of Bee Corcoran being the one who killed Stephen."

"Yeah, I dunno about that," Emma said. "If there was any evidence against Bee that made her look guilty, wouldn't Gunderson be trying to get the prosecutor after her, instead of Donnie?"

"Unless Gunderson has his own reasons for keeping her out of trouble, like being complicit in her research fraud. Maybe he doesn't want her flipping on him."

"Ooh, Molly, I like it."

"I thought you might. Anyway, when

someone's murdered, it's usually the spouse or significant other, isn't it? It wouldn't be the first time someone killed their cheating boyfriend."

"But he wasn't her boyfriend."

"So she says."

"Wait a minute, Stephen was cheating? With who?"

"I don't know. I can't think of everything. But Emma, it's Stephen we're talking about here. He was probably cheating with someone."

"Okay," Emma said. "Speaking of jealousy as a motive, how about Betty Jackson's daughter?"

"I like that idea a lot less," I said. "Verna is just a kid."

"Yeah, I agree. But Stephen dumped her and wrecked her life and now she's working this junk job and she has to see him sitting there with his new da kine."

"Exactly, Betty's daughter was working," I said. "She didn't have time to follow Stephen outside and push him over the railing. Besides, I don't want it to be Betty's daughter. I like Betty."

Emma started the car and shifted into reverse.

"I like Betty too, but everyone's got their limit, ah? In fact, I'd say it's more likely Betty killed him. Betty's daughter gave up her scholarship for Stephen Park, and then Stephen Park dumped Betty's daughter for Bee Corcoran. He broke the girl's heart and even worse, wrecked her career."

Emma peeled out into traffic inches ahead of a battered minivan.

"Eh, you think Betty Jackson is capable of murder?" Emma asked.

"No," I replied. "But neither is Donnie."

Emma swore and slammed on her brakes.

"I'll assume that wasn't directed at me," I said.

"Nah. Babooze in the minivan tailgating me. Yeah, I can't see either Betty or your husband going crazy an' killing someone. If I was making a movie called Attack of the Level-Headed Logic People, I think I'd cast Betty and Donnie in the leading roles."

"What about me? I'm a level-headed logic person."

Emma snorted.

"You? With your Italian temper?"

"Emma, you know very well I'm—"

"I know, I know, everyone thinks you're Italian but you're really Albanian."

"I'm *Albanian*, Emma...wait. That's what you just said."

Emma sped up at the yellow light and accelerated into a screeching left turn.

"Of course it is. How come you're surprised?"

"It's just that you usually get it wrong and say 'Armenian' or 'Angolan' or 'Azerbaijani' or something like that."

"Only cause it's hilarious how mad it makes you."

"I don't get mad. I just correct you. It's not the same thing. Oh, how about Niall? Betty's husband?"

"I thought he was out of town," Emma said.

"Betty *says* he's out of town. I don't want it to be him either, though. Hey, maybe Bee will be in her office,"

Emma shot me a look.

"Why do we care if Bee's in her office,

Molly? We're not going around interviewing suspects, right?"

"No, of course not. But it would be short-sighted of us to close ourselves off to readily-available information, don't you think?"

"Whoa, Molly. I said yes to seeing your new office, but talk to Bee? About what? Tell her, ha-ha, here we are, unarmed and no one knows we're here, just wanted to let you know we think you're the murderer. Hope you don't kill us now."

"Aha, so you agree Bee could be the murderer."

"Nah, I just don't wanna make her mad. She could jack us up. You seen her arms?"

"Yes, we've already been over the topic of Bee's arms. Look, I'm not saying I'm going to throw her office door open and point at her and declare, *j'accuse!*"

"Oh good. That's a relief."

"And she probably won't even be there."

"Yeah. Let's hope not." Emma gripped the steering wheel and accelerated around a slow sedan.

"But what if I just stop by to say hello

and share the sad news about my husband getting wrongfully arrested because the university's looking to blame someone for their negligence?"

Emma was already shaking her head, but I pressed on.

"And now we're spending Francesca's college fund to hire an expensive lawyer to defend him. She'll realize what she set in motion, and I think she'll consider changing her story."

"You're counting on someone you think is a murderer to have a sense of decency, Molly?"

"No, not at all. In fact—"

"Sounds like you are."

"No. Here's the thing, Emma. I tell Bee that we hired Honey Akiona to defend Donnie. Everyone knows Honey has the best investigators around. Her people are famous for finding out things the police missed. If Bee's guilty and she knows Honey Akiona is on the case, she might consider confessing before the truth comes out."

"So you're saying suppose Bee's guilty, knowing Donnie has a smart lawyer might make her think twice about trying to keep things covered up."

"Exactly."

"Yeah, I dunno. Bee had lots of opportunities to kill Park. Why would she wait to kill him at an event with so many people around?"

"To make people doubt that she did it, just like you're doubting. To make sure there are witnesses who saw the two of them getting along all lovey-dovey kissy-face in public. That's what I'd do if I wanted to kill someone."

"Good to know. Eh, you know who we should've invited today?"

"Pat!" we said in unison. Emma leaned forward and reached for her back pocket.

"You drive," I said quickly. "I'll call him. That's a great idea, Emma. He's always on the lookout for Haunted Hawaii stories for *Island Confidential*. Besides, I haven't seen him in ages."

The façade of the old Mahina Memorial Hospital was pure Victorian grimness. At the donor dinner, with the lights blazing and the conversation humming, the old edifice had felt festive. But In the gray afternoon, with black mold streaking the gray stucco, it was easy to believe the building was teeming with tormented souls.

"So, this is where Miss Constance is supposedly floating around?" I asked Emma. "Pushing people off balconies?"

"Sometimes she just scares 'em to death," Emma said. "Or makes 'em go crazy. Or derails their train. Eh Molly, where do I park?"

"College of Commerce isn't in the main building," I said. "Dan told me we're around the back."

Emma cut over from the main driveway to a narrow access path that snaked around the side of the old hospital building. We descended as we made our way around, so by the time we reached the back of the hospital we were a good two stories lower than the front. Emma stopped in front of what looked like an ancient loading dock. Wide bay doors were boarded up with plywood. The hospital had its best face to the street. Viewed from the back, it looked like a strong wind could blow it apart.

My glasses fogged up the minute I stepped out of the car, thanks to Mahina's humidity. Downhill to our left, half-embedded in the jungle that had overtaken the untended edges of the property, was a boxy building. It was a dirty white, and completely bereft of Victorian adornment.

"Darn it," I said. "We don't get a fabulous Victorian building. That thing looks like it could've been built in the thirties as part of the EUR."

"What's the EUR?" Emma asked. "Something bad, it sounds like."

"An un-fabulous suburb of Rome. Built by Benito Mussolini."

"I think you're approaching this with a very negative attitude, Molly. Eh, is that where it happened?" Emma pointed upward.

Around twenty or thirty feet above us a balcony jutted from the main hospital building, surrounded by a low railing. I quickly looked down at my feet to see what I was standing on. An old concrete pad, half-buried in charcoal-gray dirt and dried leaves.

"It looks higher up than I remember." I looked up at the balcony again, and down at the ground.

Floomp. I wished I could forget the sound. "Well, we don't have all day," I said brightly. "Let's go find my office."

"Eh, careful, ah, you two!"

Emma and I looked up to see a young woman peering over the railing.

"Honey?" I called up.

"Stay right there, I'm coming around."

"What do you think Honey Akiona is doing here?" I said to Emma. "It must have something to do with Donnie's case. I hope so, anyway."

"You tell her about what Betty's daughter said?" Emma asked. "About our dean talking with the prosecutor?"

"No. Donnie asked me not to get involved."

"What? And you listened to him?"

"Look, he specifically said to me, don't contact her, just let her do her job."

"Wouldn't she do her job better if she knew about the university wanting to frame him for Stephen Park's murder, so they can minimize their own liability?"

"If you ask me, yes. But Donnie thinks I'll go blundering in and mess everything up."

"Yeah I can see his point," Emma said as Honey Akiona came around the corner of the building. "Donnie's right. You shouldn't say anything to her."

"What?"

"But that doesn't mean I can't tell her."

"Ah. Well, tell her whatever you like. As long as it's clear you didn't hear it from me."

"You got it. Eh, Honey, howzit?"

Honey Akiona cut a striking figure. Her leather pumps boosted her to six feet tall, and a navy-blue pantsuit flattered her Junoesque contours. She had cut her dark hair to chin length, where it hung in a glossy bob. She embraced Emma first, planting Emma's face directly in her impressive bosom. I got a hug too, and then we got down to business.

"Professor, you get my messages?"

"Messages?" I pulled my phone out and saw the icon for un-played voice mail messages in the corner of my screen. "Ooh. Sorry about that. I've kind of been behind on my voice mail."

"I was trying to set up a meeting with you to go over your statement, see if you could remember anything else about that night. But now that you're here, you got some time to talk?"

"Sure," I said.

"I get something," Emma said eagerly.

"Professor Nakamura. Were you at the event?"

"Nah. Molly only went cause her dean couldn't make it. But you gotta hear this. My dean, Gunderson, and the prosecutor are framing Donnie so the university doesn't have to pay Stephen Park's parents."

As the three of us stood in the chilly shadow of the old hospital building, Emma told Honey Akiona about the overheard conversation between the arts and sciences dean and the county prosecutor. I was impressed by Emma's memory for detail. I couldn't think of a single thing to add to her account.

Honey listened with her arms folded,

staring at the ground as Emma spoke. She seemed to find the news distasteful, but not surprising.

"I suspected something wasn't right," she said, when Emma had finished. "Pang won't touch a case unless it's an easy win, or there's something in it for him. Good thing I came out here when I did."

"Honey, what are you doing out here?" I asked.

"Taking measurements and pictures. That way if the university tries to fix that railing after the fact, I have visual proof of the way it was before they changed it."

"Wouldn't the police have pictures of the scene?" Emma asked.

"I've found it's better not to rely on someone else." Honey was looking at a spot on the ground about ten feet away from where we were standing. The leaves and dirt had been washed away and one patch was lighter than the surrounding concrete, as if it had been bleached. It was a little disorienting to see it in the daylight, but I still had a pretty good idea of what we were looking at.

"Is that where it happened?" I asked quietly.

Honey nodded.

"Oh, by the way—"

"You remembered something else?" Honey asked.

"Well, not exactly. But Emma and I were talking, and we have a theory."

"Oh." Honey's enthusiasm had vanished.

"Molly," Emma said, "maybe now's not the time—"

"We think you should look into Bee Corcoran," I persisted.

"No, not we," Emma interjected.

"She has two possible motives," I went on. "One, she was committing research fraud and Stephen found out. Two, he was cheating on her."

"I agree something was weird about Bee's research results," Emma said. "But the other stuff, we were just kicking some ideas around."

"Did you see them arguing?" Honey asked. "Corcoran and Park?"

"I didn't see them arguing, no."

"You got any proof he was cheating?"

"Well, not proof exactly, but—"

"Do you know who he was cheating with?"

"Well, no, but he—"

"Are you sure Corcoran and Park were romantically involved to begin with?" Honey asked.

"They came to the dinner together," I said, a little defensively. "Bee actually told me she and Stephen weren't an item, but that was after he was already dead. Maybe she was lying to me to throw me off the scent."

Honey nodded.

"Okay. Well, I'll look into it," she reached into her briefcase to pull out a business card. "Listen, I gotta go, but please call me if you remember anything else."

"Honey, wait."

She turned around.

"You said the prosecutor would go after a case if it was an easy win, or something else. What is the something else?"

"The usual. Reward his friends, punish his enemies, or get a big donation for his re-election campaign."

Emma and I remained standing on the spot after Honey had left.

"Molly," Emma asked, "what is wrong with you?"

"What do you mean? You were on board with the Bee theory."

"Yeah, when we're talking about it between ourselves. But you say it out loud in front of a real lawyer and it sounds totally meshuggeneh."

"If there's nothing to it then there's nothing to it. But I don't think there's any harm in sharing our thoughts with her. Dang it. She probably does think I'm nuts now, doesn't she?"

"You still wanna go see your office or what?" Emma asked.

"Dan said we have the top floor," I said as we started down the hill.

Chapter Twenty-Seven

"I HOPE my new office doesn't look out this way," I said as we made our way along the narrow walkway through the trees. "I don't want to have to see where Stephen died."

"Molly. Don't you live next to a graveyard?"

"Another reason why I don't want to stare death in the face all day."

"You know this place was a *hospital*. Literally tons of people died here. And don't call me out for saying 'literally'. I do mean literally, cause all you need is ten or twenty people to make a ton. Even less if it's a bunch of fat guys."

"I know Stephen wasn't the first person

to die here, Emma, I'm not an idiot. But he's the first person I know personally who died here. It's different."

The building entrance was a soap-green wooden door. Unlike the double doors at the entrance to the main hospital, this was not at all grand. Emma pushed the door open and I followed her. Inside it was surprisingly bright. I looked up to see that the center of the building was an atrium, open all the way up to an expansive skylight.

"This is like that hotel I just stayed in for my conference in Phoenix," Emma said. "You step out of your room and there's like this low wall about waist high, and like fifty feet below is the lobby."

"It sounds dangerous," I said. "Wouldn't it be easy to fall right over?"

"No one died when I was there."

"Well, here's my new daily workout," I said as we started up the steps.

"Ho, this is pretty nice. *Helloooo!*"

"Emma, don't shout."

"What? You afraid I'm gonna wake up the ghosts?"

"No, I'm afraid your voice is going to destabilize the building like the Tacoma Narrows bridge and it's going to tumble down and crush us to death."

"Hello!" Came a man's voice. From the top of the stairwell, I could see the top of a shaved head.

"Pat!" Emma picked up speed and bounded up the steps. I did my best to keep up, but I quickly lost sight of her. Emma's canoe paddling keeps her extremely fit. By the time I had reached the top floor I felt like I was breathing sandpaper.

Pat was attired after his usual fashion, in black boots, grubby jeans, and a battered flannel shirt over a Joy Division t-shirt. He's pale, wiry, and tall. Emma is short, brown, and built for power. Standing side by side they look like an illustration of Diversity of the Human Species.

"This is it?" I exclaimed, after I'd exchanged a quick hug with Pat. "Just a landing and a couple doors?"

I backed away from the railing.

"You should stay away from the railing,"

Emma advised helpfully. "You're scared of heights."

"Yes, thank you for reminding me. Except there's not a lot of space up here."

"Hey Molly, sorry to hear about Donnie," Pat said.

"Thanks. It's been pretty stressful. Have you heard anything down at Mahina PD?"

Pat shrugged. "If it makes you feel any better, it doesn't seem like anyone there really thinks Donnie killed anyone."

"Eh, Pat, you know anything about this building?" Emma asked.

"I didn't even know it was here until today," I added. "Emma, you're making me nervous leaning over the railing."

"I'm not gonna fall over," she said.

Pat was snapping photos with his cell phone. "I'm gonna come out and say it's definitely haunted. At least for the purpose of my next installment of Mysterious Mahina."

"I thought your thing was called Haunted Hawaii," Emma said.

"It was, until the Mahina Chamber of Commerce started advertising in *Island*

Confidential. They wanted something more distinctive and Mahina-centric. So now my column is called Mysterious Mahina."

"Is this the famous firewall between editorial and advertising that we're always hearing about?" I asked.

"Give me a break. I'm just trying to make up the difference between teaching intro comp and making a living wage." Pat tried the handle to Room 310; it was locked. He turned back from the door and looked around. "Hey. Where's Emma?"

I had a flash of panic, imagining Emma tipping quietly over the railing and plummeting to her death. Fortunately, Emma strolled out of the bathroom at that moment as the sound of gurgling water reverberated in the walls.

"Here she is," I said. "How's the bathroom?"

She shrugged. "Clean. Unisex bathroom though. So it's probably not going to stay clean with you an' three guys in your department. Hey Pat, guess what—"

"I'm going to go look at the bathroom." I

jerked my head toward the bathroom. "Emma, you want to show me around?"

"Yeah, let me show you around," she said and followed me in.

Unlike the landing outside, the bathroom was humid and poorly-lit. A small globe fixture and a dusty breadbox-sized window were the only sources of light. A cloudy mirror was mounted over a cantilevered celadon-green sink You'd think the combination of the dim light and the aged mirror would be flattering, but a quick glimpse of my reflection showed the opposite. Not only did I look waxy and undead, but my hair was going wild in the humidity. It was like every strand had decided it hated every other strand and they were bristling as far from one another as they could.

"Do you think these are the original floor tiles?" I asked.

The floor was covered in 2-inch hexagonal tiles in the same celadon green as the sink, the walls, and the rust-speckled metal stalls. The tiles were cracked and chipped, but clean.

"Molly, why are you acting so weird? I know you didn't bring me in here to talk about floor tiles."

"I thought you were going to tell Pat what Betty's daughter overheard. About your dean trying to talk the prosecutor into framing Donnie for Stephen's death."

"Yeah, I was, so?"

"Anything you tell him will end up in *Island Confidential.*"

"And then?"

"And then it could mess up whatever Honey might be planning. Maybe she doesn't want to tip them off that she knows what they're up to."

Emma sighed.

"Yeah, okay. Eh, check out this magic mirror, all blurry. Makes me look like a frickin' movie star."

Emma flicked her hair over her shoulder and sauntered out. I followed her out to the sunny landing.

"So, let's have a look at my choices," I said. "Which office will I least regret choosing?"

"Pat, tell her which office has the least ghosts living in it," Emma said.

"The *fewest* ghosts," I wanted to say, but didn't. You'd think people would appreciate helpful corrections like this, but I've found they don't.

Room 310 was on the wall to the left. On the right was the door to the restroom. In front of me were three doors in the same hospital green as the front door and the bathroom. They were labeled 311, 312, and 314.

"So what have you found out about this place?" I tried the door handles. But the offices were all locked.

"I have some good stuff on the main building." Pat had his hand braced on the railing.

"Pat, don't lean on that," I said. "You don't know how much termite damage there is."

He picked his hand up and folded his arms but didn't move away from the railing.

"They put in a lot of effort and expense considering it was a TB hospital in a territorial backwater," he said. "They got

Carrara marble for the floors. Think about shipping marble from Italy to Hawaii. The family that financed this wanted the hospital to be a showplace. To put Mahina on the map. I found this quote. Hang on."

Pat brought something up on his phone.

"Here it is. 'Fair Mahina will outshine not only Honolulu, but will grow to rival the great capitals of the world.'"

"Great capitals of the world?" Emma snorted. "Mahina? Pat, you should do a series called Delusional Rich Idiots of History."

"So what was this building used for then?" I looked up at the skylight, which from the top floor looked enormous. It was rectangular, around eight by ten feet, of plain frosted glass. Four muntins formed a large rectangle in the middle and little squares in each corner. "Dan thought it might be nurses' quarters."

"Was it the nuthouse?" Emma walked over and punched my shoulder playfully. "Cause that'd be appropriate."

"This building was actually the Inebriate Asylum," Pat said. "Old-timey rehab."

"Eh, no look at me li'dat," Emma protested.

"What? I didn't say anything about you reeking of beer in the middle of the day," Pat said.

"I took the breathalyzer before we drove here, ah, Molly?"

"You have a breathalyzer?" Pat asked.

"In my glove box," Emma declared proudly. "Don't leave home without it."

Pat shook his head and recommenced taking pictures. Pat never drinks alcohol, and he never talks about it. And I've never asked him.

"It's true," I said. "She was below the limit. Emma won't tell me where she got that aftermarket liver installed, but I want one. Do you hear sirens?"

The sirens got louder, and then seemed to stop somewhere below us.

"Sounds like it's on that side," Emma said. "Behind those doors."

"Only one thing to do," Pat reached into his back pocket and hunched over the handle of the door marked 312. "Molly, you might want to turn away."

"From what? I see nothing."

It took Pat less than a minute to do whatever he was doing to the door. He stood up and pushed it open. The room was around ten by twelve feet. Two large crank-out windows admitted the hot afternoon sun. The walls were the familiar hospital green, and the linoleum square flooring was a checkerboard of green and beige. A putty-colored file cabinet, frosted with rust, was the only piece of furniture.

At first I thought the windows didn't have any kind of covering, but on closer inspection I could see yellowed Venetian blinds that had been pulled all the way up. The view was of the back of the main hospital building. From this angle I saw the hospital walls were streaked with black mold and the windows were black and dusty. If I pressed my face to the glass and looked down, I could see the terrace where Stephen spent his last living moments. Further to the left, nearly out of my line of vision, was the rickety wooden staircase leading from the emergency exit down to the ground.

"You get to look at that all day?" Pat asked me. "Depressing."

"I'll get used to it," I said, stepping back from the window. "Besides, if you look off to the right you can see trees."

"Over there!" Emma's face was pressed to the window. We rushed over to see an ambulance pulling away from the side of the building and out onto the main road. It gave a single whoop of its siren as it slowly moved out of our sight.

"I hope whoever it is, is okay," I said. "It's always kind of disturbing to hear an ambulance and imagine—"

"Hello," a voice echoed from somewhere in the building. "Anyone inside?"

Chapter Twenty-Eight

"SECURITY," the voice yelled as we scrambled to leave the office. "Anyone here? Gotta clear the building."

Pat quickly locked the door behind us and the three of us went thundering down the stairs. Pat's long legs could take the steps three or four at a time, but Emma still got to the ground floor first. I, of course, brought up the rear. The ground floor was abandoned when I got there. I eventually found Pat, Emma, and a security guard outside, next to Emma's car.

"Was someone hurt or what?" Emma was asking him.

The young man frowned.

"I not supposed to say nothing, Auntie."

"We should probably go," I said. "We can come back later—"

"Cannot," the young man said evenly. "Gotta wait for the police."

"I really have to get home," I objected. I was starting to feel pressure in my chest, and mentally kicked myself for not having brought my breast pump. Unfortunately, I didn't have my car with me. And Emma and Pat didn't seem like they were going anywhere.

Just as I had made up my mind to walk home, a familiar silhouette came lumbering around the corner.

Detective Ka`imi Medeiros.

He nodded to the three of us by way of greeting, and again to the young guard to dismiss him.

"Mister Flanagan," he said. "Professor Barda. Professor Nakamura. What brings you here today?"

"My dean told me to come here. So I did." I knew Medeiros thought I was a loose cannon, so maybe he'd be impressed by my compliance with authority.

"Your dean. Is that Geoffrey Gunderson?" Medeiros asked.

"No, Dean Gunderson is Arts and Sciences. My dean is Dan Watanabe in the College of Commerce. Our new offices are in that building over there. Dan asked me to go in and pick the office I wanted, so that's what I'm doing."

"How about you, Professor Nakamura?" He asked Emma. "What are you doing here?"

"I'm helping Molly make good choices," Emma replied.

"I'm doing research for my Mysterious Mahina series," Pat said before Medeiros had a chance to address him. "For Island Confidential."

"Did any of you see anything?" Medeiros asked. No one answered him. If we told Medeiros we had seen an ambulance pulling away, we might have to tell him that we saw it from the window of room 312, which would then bring up the awkward question of how we got into room 312.

"We heard a siren," Emma said. "Then da

kine came in the building and yelled at us to get out."

"Detective, what is this about?" I asked. "Was someone hurt?"

"That's what we're trying..."

His eyes flicked to my shirt for a microsecond. He blinked.

"Okay. If you remember anything, any of you, please get in touch."

Detective Medeiros turned abruptly and walked off.

"What just happened?" I asked. "What did I say?"

"Probably time for you to get home," Emma said. "Look at your shirt."

Pat had his back turned to us and appeared to be examining his phone with great interest.

I looked down to see two dark-blue milk stains spreading on the front of my shirt.

Chapter Twenty-Nine

THE THREE OF us watched Detective Medeiros disappear around the corner of the old hospital building.

"What's the matter with him?" I asked. "Doesn't he see hacked-up bodies every day? I can't believe I scared him off with a little breast—"

"Aah!" Pat interrupted, clamping his hands over his ears.

"You're not a hacked-up body to Medeiros," Emma said. "You're Donnie's wife. I think it's different. Eh, you need a ride home?"

I looked down at my stained blouse.

"Do you mind if we kill fifteen or twenty

minutes before we go? I'd like to get home after Margaret leaves. I'd rather Donnie saw me like this than Margaret.

"What, you think Margaret cares about your milk stains?" Emma asked. "Isn't she there exactly to do baby stuff?"

"Yeah, but she used to be my student. That makes it more embarrassing for some reason. Hey, where did Pat go?"

"I dunno. Oh, here he comes. Eh, babooze, couldn't handle a little grownup conversation about breast milk?"

Pat was sprinting up from the direction opposite to where Medeiros had gone.

"I'm going inside before they lock up the building," he panted.

"I like come," Emma said eagerly. "Molly, you can wait down here if you don't feel like keeping up."

"What? I can keep up. I'll just follow you guys. I don't want to just stand here oozing for twenty minutes. Where are we going?"

Pat led us around the other side of the hospital building, across an overgrown courtyard, through a splintery door, into a dark stairwell. Pat and Emma then bounded up what seemed like 17,000 flights of creaky stairs while I huffed and puffed behind them. Finally, Pat pushed open a door and we emerged into the end of a hallway.

"Sorry, Molly," he said. "I didn't want us to risk getting stuck in the elevator."

"No, it's fine," I wheezed, bracing my hands on my knees. "It's good. I can use the exercise."

"So how come we're here?" Emma asked.

"Molly, are you okay?" Pat bent down and tried to look at my face. I nodded, not wanting to waste valuable oxygen by speaking.

"I managed to talk to the security guard before he left," Pat said. "He was in pretty bad shape."

"Why?" I heard Emma ask. With my hands clutching my knees, I studied the floor and tried to control my breath so I wouldn't hyperventilate. The flooring here on the upper level was linoleum, just like in the Inebriates' Asylum out back. The fancy marble was reserved for the lower floors that the public would see. Or maybe marble was too heavy for anything but the ground floor.

"He told me he was walking around the building, and thought he saw something shining in the bushes," Pat said. "He went to check it out and saw it was a woman's blonde hair. That's when he called the police."

"Was it a wig?" Emma asked.

"Emma," I wheezed, "why would he call the police on a wig?"

"Cause maybe it was a *stolen* wig," she countered.

"Who would steal a wig and then hide it in the bushes? That doesn't make any sense."

"Sorry to have to tell you this," Pat said, "but the blonde hair was actually attached to a person. Sad to say."

I finally caught my breath and stood up.

"Do they know who it was?" I asked.

"He said she was a haole lady, and she was wearing what he called one of those white doctor coats."

Emma and I looked at each other.

"Bee!" we exclaimed.

"Yeah, that's what I thought too," Pat said.

"How do you know who Bee Corcoran is?" I asked him.

"Emma's been keeping me up to date," Pat said. "Good thing you have an alibi, Molly. In case it really was Bee down there."

"Me? Why would I want to hurt Bee?"

"Molly, you can't stand Bee," Emma said.

"Emma, Shh!"

"What? All the doors on this hallway are closed. No can hear me."

"You have no idea how loud your voice is," I whispered. "Anyway, it's not true. I don't hate Bee. Not at all. I *like* Bee."

"Even when she gives you unsolicited weight-loss advice?" Pat asked.

"She's only trying to be helpful," I said. "However misguided her efforts may be."

"The directory says her lab's on this floor," Pat said. "Should be about halfway down on the left."

"Emma, what did you tell him?" I asked.

Emma shrugged.

We followed Pat to Bee's lab. No need to do any lock-picking here; the door was unlocked. Pat walked right in, and we followed him.

The lab smelled like cedar shavings and mothballs, with a hint of stinky mammal. Mounted on the wall to our left was a grid of cages, each of which contained a single rat. On the far side of the lab, floor-to-ceiling horizontal blinds clattered softly, stirred by a breeze. Hazy sunlight filtered through the slats.

"Hello?" A slender young man with wide-spaced blue eyes emerged from behind something that looked like a refrigerator. He was wearing a blue t-shirt and jeans, and carrying a large cardboard Amazon box. Draped over the top of the box was a white lab coat. I quickly folded my arms over my milk-stained t-shirt and ducked behind Pat.

"Oh, hey," the young man said. "Did you guys move my stuff?"

"We just got here," Pat said. "What stuff?"

"Someone moved this," the young man nodded at the box in his arms. "Looks like everything's in there, though. No big."

"We're looking for Dr. Corcoran," Emma said. "Is she around?"

"I haven't seen her today," the boy replied.

"You work here?" Pat asked.

"Not anymore." He rested the box on the edge of a nearby counter. "I just came to get my things and say goodbye to my little buddies here. Refill their water, which *someone* forgot to do today." He nodded toward the white rats in their cages. Most of the animals were sleeping, but here and there a pink nose twitched through the metal mesh of the cage. Each rat had a water bottle mounted on the cage, and each bottle was filled to the top with clear water.

Maybe that's what I needed. A water bottle as tall as I was, mounted next to the glider chair in the master bedroom. Then I wouldn't have to beg people to bring me water when I nursed Francesca. I could just lick the ball bearing at the end of the metal tube.

"We'll just leave Dr. Corcoran a note, then," Emma said. We all stepped aside to let the boy pick up his box and leave.

As soon as he was gone, we separated and began poking around. I went over to open the blinds.

"I'll help," Pat said as he came over. "This window is way too big for this heavy of blinds. They should've used vertical ones."

"I never liked vertical blinds," I remarked, watching Pat manipulate the strings carefully to avoid the blinds going crooked. "They remind me of depressing grad-school apartments. But I guess I see the point of them."

"A balcony?" Emma exclaimed behind us.

"Pretty deluxe," I said.

"Yeah, not in a Biosafety Level 2 lab," Emma said. "There's not supposed to be a window that opens to the outside like —whoa!"

Emma and I stepped back as Pat finished lifting the blinds. A pair of tall French doors opened onto a narrow balcony surrounded by rusty metalwork railing. The center part of the railing had been broken through. An unobstructed breeze blew in, which would have been pleasant if we weren't standing on the fourth floor next to a busted railing where someone had probably just fallen to her death.

"What's down there?" I asked Pat. He'd placed one foot on the balcony and was holding on to the door frame with one hand and was leaning out. I could barely stand to look at him.

"Down there is where they found her," Pat said. "There's the road that goes around the hospital, and I can see a piece of yellow tape from here. Too bad my ghost cam wasn't positioned to catch what happened."

"Ghost cam?" I asked.

Pat came back inside and lowered the blinds carefully.

"I put a camera out to catch supernatural activity," he said. "But I set it up directly in the front. That's where the building looks the best."

"Do you really think that was Bee down there?" I asked. "The person that they found? Bee Corcoran is dead?"

Pat perched on a countertop and folded his arms.

"Yeah, I think so."

"That boy who was just in here," Emma said. "Think he did it? He said it was his last day here."

"You mean she fired him," I asked. "And for revenge, he pushed her out the window?"

"Yeah, I don't know," Pat said. "If he killed her, would he come back later to get his things?"

"Maybe to throw us off," Emma said. "Pun intended."

"That's a terrible pun, Emma," I said. "You're right, Pat. He was pretty calm for someone who had just murdered someone earlier in the day."

"Probably a psychopath," Emma said. "There's a lot of 'em out there, you know."

"Hey, I teach creative writing," Pat said. "You don't have to tell me about psychopaths. I don't know what's worse, the number of guys who write stories about murdering some girl who rejected them, or the fact that they all think they're being original and edgy. Okay, as long as we're here, I'm going to get some pictures."

"Here?" I asked. "Why?"

But Pat already had his phone out.

"You never know what's going to come in handy later," he said.

"Shouldn't we go?" I asked. "I don't want to be here when Detective Medeiros figures out their body is Bee and comes back here."

"Hey, look" Emma called out from a corner of the room. "The phone."

A black push-button landline phone sat on the countertop, the receiver lying off the hook. A crumpled paper towel lay next to it.

"There's nothing connecting it to the wall," I said.

"That's right," Emma said. "No wire. How does that fit in? Hmm. Murderer comes in, steals the phone wire so no one can call for help, pushes Bee out the window, closes the blinds, and runs away."

"Speaking of running away," I said, "can we go? And how does it help to steal a telephone cord? I'm sure Bee has a cell phone. Had."

"Eh Molly," Emma said, "I guess our theory doesn't work so good anymore, ah?"

"Yeah, whatever. No one left any

fingerprints, right?" I asked as the door closed behind us.

"We have an eyewitness who can place all three of us here," Pat said. "I'm not sure fingerprints will make a difference."

"Oh. Right," I said.

"So, still think Bee killed Stephen?" Emma asked me as we followed Pat out.

"Molly," Pat asked, "you thought Bee killed Stephen Park?"

"No. Maybe." We followed Pat to the end of the hallway and into the emergency exit stairwell.

"Are Stephen's parents still on island?" Emma asked. "What did they think of Bee?"

"I don't know," I said. "I don't think *they* killed her though, if that's what you're asking. It doesn't seem like the kind of thing they'd do."

"A lot of murderers don't seem like murderers," Pat said. "You'd be surprised."

The stairs seemed a lot shorter on the way down than they had on the way up. But that might have been because we were all running.

It didn't really hit me until we were downstairs, standing around Emma's car.

"Oh my gosh," I said. "Bee Corcoran is dead."

"If it is Bee," Pat said. "But yeah, who else would it be? Blonde hair, wearing a lab coat?"

"I wonder if it was suicide," I said. "How sad."

"Why would Bee commit suicide?" Emma demanded. "She just got the life sciences research award."

"It doesn't work like that, Emma," Pat said. "You never know what kind of things people are struggling with in secret."

"I know one thing," I said.

Pat and Emma looked at me.

"Bee is transgender. Was."

"Nah!" Emma exclaimed.

"How did you know?" Pat asked.

"Stephen told me."

"How come you never told me?" Emma demanded. "I can't believe you kept it a secret. You're usually such a blabbermouth."

"It wasn't my place to say anything. If she wanted people to know, she would have told them. And you have no evidence for your claim that I'm a blabbermouth."

"Why did Stephen tell you about it?" Pat asked.

"Oh, probably to make sure I knew how interesting and awesome Bee was. I'm sure in his mind being trans gives you extra 'cool' points or something."

"Like how he went around fooling people into thinking he was half-Korean cause his last name was Park?" Emma asked.

"Yeah, that sounds about right," Pat said. "Anything to strike the right pose."

"I wonder who's gonna get her lab space," Emma said. "Her lab's got at least twenty percent more square footage than mines."

"I know you two think Bee led a charmed life," Pat said, "But Molly, if what you just told us is true…seriously, what would you do if you woke up tomorrow in a man's body?"

"Go to HR and demand my thirty percent raise," I said.

"Helicopter!" Emma raised her arms and rotated her hips.

"How about both at once?" I said. "That'd make an impression."

Pat sighed.

"Okay. I gotta go. Enjoy your straight cis privilege, ladies."

We watched Pat disappear into the hospital building's late-afternoon shadows.

"Wow. Tough crowd," I said.

"He should know I was just kidding about the helicopter thing," Emma said. "I can't even hula-hoop."

Chapter Thirty

MARGARET'S CAR was still in front of my house when Emma dropped me off. Donnie wasn't home yet. I tried sneaking around the back. My plan was to get to the laundry room and grab a fresh shirt before Margaret saw me. But as soon as I stepped onto the back deck, there she was. She was sitting in one of the uncomfortable teak folding chairs, holding Francesca on her lap. I quickly crossed my arms to cover my chest, but as soon as I got closer I forgot about my stained shirt. Margaret's eyes were red and shining. She'd been crying.

I quickly took Francesca from her and

held the baby close to me. Our hedge had grown high enough to block the view of the graveyard, so I couldn't see it. It was a small favor. This day was already weird enough.

"Margaret? Are you okay?

I sat next to her and popped the baby under my shirt. Francesca latched on with gusto, quickly relieving the painful pressure in my chest. Exactly the kind of thing we in the College of Commerce like to call a "win-win."

Margaret shook her head.

"I'm so sorry, Professor," she sniffled.

"About what? The baby's okay. The house seems fine. What's going on?"

She looked at me with her red-rimmed eyes.

"I'm leaving."

"You what? Why? Did you want to talk about the pay? Maybe we could—"

"I'm moving back to the mainland," she said.

"What? Where on the mainland?"

"Oregon."

"But what about the CPA exam?"

"I can take the CPA exam and practice there."

"Oh. You're sure about this?"

She nodded.

"Okay. Well, if that's what you want to do, then I'm happy for you. We'll just have to adjust and plan for a smooth transition. When are you planning to leave?"

"Tonight."

"*Tonight?*"

Margaret flinched.

"Sorry, Margaret, I didn't mean to raise my voice. I was surprised, that's all. I honestly don't know what we'll do without you."

"I'm so sorry," Margaret repeated.

"No, no, I'm not saying it to make you feel guilty. You've been wonderful with Francesca, and we're going to miss you. That's what I wanted to say. And this is all so sudden."

"I'll miss Francesca," Margaret sniffled. She was staring out at the hedge, in the direction of the graveyard. "I'll miss Hawaii. I'm so sorry, I know this puts you in a bad spot."

"Well, is there anyone you know who might be able to take the job?" I asked. ""Do you remember the young man you told me about, who was looking for a job? You said he loved animals?"

"Keola?" She turned to look at me. "We're moving to Oregon together."

"Ah. Okay. So that won't work."

"He said if he couldn't find another job by the last day of work, he was going to leave the islands. His last day of work was today."

A little advance warning would have been nice, I thought.

"Is the job situation any better on the mainland?" I asked.

"Oh, the job market's much better there. He's already got something lined up. With a food safety testing lab. And Hawaii's the worst state for CPAs when you count housing costs and available jobs. We're number 51."

"How do we rank fifty-one when there are only fifty states?" I asked.

"Washington, DC."

Margaret burst into tears. I hesitated, debating whether to give her a hug. Neither of us really wanted that, I decided. I went inside and got her a box of tissues.

Chapter Thirty-One

DONNIE, baby Francesca, and I arrived at Honey Akiona's office exactly at two o'clock the next day. Honey had called Donnie to request a meeting and had asked him to bring me along.

Honey had moved her practice to a new office, on the bottom floor of an early 20th-century frontier-style building downtown. It was close to the Pair-O-Dice, but one street nearer to the bayfront.

Her assistant let us in to her office and we waited for a few moments. Honey finally came in, holding a manila folder.

"Aw, *cute*, the baby." Honey gave

Francesca a smile and rubbed the top of her fuzzy head.

"Bah!" Francesca replied with a gummy grin.

"We didn't have anyone to watch her," I said as I pulled the baby to my chest and draped my shirt over her. "Excuse us. The baby's hungry."

"No worries. This won't take long. We got a situation." She dropped the folder on her desk and sat down. "Bee Corcoran is dead."

I nudged Donnie's foot, a nonverbal "I told you so." When I told Donnie what had happened, he had been infuriatingly skeptical. The body was probably a homeless person; there were any number of reasons Bee might not have been in her lab when we visited; the balcony railing had probably rusted out long ago.

I wasn't happy Bee was dead, of course, but maybe next time Donnie wouldn't be so quick to dismiss my conclusions.

"This could be a problem," Honey continued. "Bee Corcoran could confirm when you left the table, so you could say it's to your advantage to have her out of the way."

"Is someone saying I killed Bee Corcoran?" Donnie asked.

"Pang might try to go in that direction," Honey said. "Donnie Gonsalves murders his wife's ex-boyfriend out of jealousy, then kills a key witness. Pang solves two murders for the price of one and banks a big favor for the university."

"What do you mean, a favor for the university?" he asked Honey.

"Stephen Park's parents are suing the university for Stephen's death. The university would prefer to shift the blame somewhere else. Like to you, for example. Where were you yesterday morning?"

"I was at the Drive-Inn," Donnie said. "From seven in the morning until about three."

"How did Bee die?" I asked.

Honey opened the folder and traced her finger down the top piece of paper.

"No official cause of death yet, but probably head trauma."

"From the fall?"

Honey stared at me.

"Do you know anything about this, Professor?"

I had no reason to keep anything from Honey. I told her everything I could remember from the previous day. She seemed to be more open-minded than Donnie had been.

"We didn't do anything wrong, did we? I didn't think we were trespassing or anything." I stole a sidelong glance at Donnie.

"You say the door was unlocked?"

"To Bee's lab? Yes."

"You heard that someone had died, and her description sounded like your colleague. You went to her office—"

"Her lab," I corrected Honey. "Just to check on her."

"You went to your colleague's workspace, to check on her. The door was unlocked. Your actions were reasonable. What about the boy who was there? Any idea who he is?"

"I'm not sure. But I think he's Margaret Adams's friend Keola. Margaret said he had just left his job, and the boy in the lab told us it was his last day of work."

"Margaret Adams?" Honey raised her eyebrows.

"That's right, I forgot. She's your classmate. She's been watching our daughter in the mornings."

"She never went for her CPA? I thought she'd be working for one of the Big Four by now."

"She's studying for the CPA exam. In fact, she reads her study flashcards to Francesca. Puts her right to sleep. Well, she did, anyway. She—"

"Professor. Does the boy in the lab have a last name?"

"Oh. Sorry. If it's the same person, I think his name is Keola Shiner."

"You didn't tell me all this last night," Donnie said.

"I didn't think of it. I just remembered that Margaret had told me that Bee fired him from her lab."

"Fired?" Honey asked. "Interesting."

"He must be on the mainland by now," I said. "Margaret said they were going to fly out last night. That's why we have the baby today. We don't have anyone to watch her any more. I guess you don't have Margaret's forwarding address."

"No," Honey said. "I'd appreciate it if you have it."

I pulled out my phone to search for Margaret's contact information.

"I can email it to you."

"Just write it down." Honey pushed a legal pad across the desk to me. Then, in response to my questioning look, "I like to be on the safe side. You know what they say. Email like the whole world's watching. And Mr. Gonsalves, we're going to need to contact some other witnesses to your whereabouts yesterday, besides your employees. Customers, anyone else who might've seen you. You understand."

As I was driving back home with Donnie, Francesca in her car seat in the back, my phone rang. It was Serena, the dean's secretary.

"Molly," she said, "You never got back to Dan about what office you want. I gotta get the assignments to Facilities by the end of the week. They just called to remind me cause they're gonna put up the signs outside your door that's why."

"Right. I did go over there yesterday, but—"

"Yesterday?"

"Yes."

"I heard someone found a dead body in the main building yesterday. You see anything?"

"I didn't see a dead body," I said, "but a security guard came into the building and chased us, me, out."

"Nah! Really?"

"I'll go back today and choose my office. Oh, what should I do if the doors are locked?"

"Call security and get 'em to let you in," Serena replied. "And call me or email me as soon as you decide. So I can cross it off my list. Don't try to tell Dan. He's about a thousand emails behind."

When Serena had hung up, Donnie said, "It's okay. I'll take the baby."

"That's nice of you to offer, but I don't really feel good about having her at the

Drive-Inn with all of the open flames and knives and things."

"Well, in our defense, no one's died at the Drive-Inn in the past week."

"Yeah, good point. Okay, you and Francesca go into the Drive-Inn and try to figure out who came in to buy breakfast yesterday. Make sure you have a rock-solid alibi."

"Do you want us to go with you?" Donnie asked. "I don't like the idea of you going to the old hospital alone. You don't know who's hanging around there."

"My office isn't in the actual hospital."

"It's not?"

"Nope. We're out back. In the Inebriate Asylum."

"Really?"

"Yes. Really."

"So are you going to tell your students to come to your office hours in the Inebriate Asylum?"

"That's exactly what I'll tell them. In fact, thank you for reminding me. I need to put it on my syllabus.

"Molly?" Donnie watched the road as he talked, so I knew he was serious now.

"Yes?"

"Please don't go investigating anything."

"I won't."

"Molly, I'm serious. Two people have already died up there. We don't know who might be hanging around."

"I'll get Emma to come with me."

Donnie gave me a sideways glance.

"Good. I think."

Chapter Thirty-Two

DONNIE DROPPED me off at home. I called Emma, but her phone went straight to voice mail. My friend-finder app showed Emma in the middle of Mahina Bay. Darn it. She was out paddling and might not be back for hours.

I dialed Pat Flanagan's number. He, it turned out, was in town, and available. I hopped into my Thunderbird and drove over to the old hospital building. It was closer to my house than the main campus, I realized. One of these days, when we got our childcare situation squared away, I might even be able to walk to work.

I parked in front of the main hospital

building, in the shade of a strip of jungle on the mauka (uphill) side. It would have been closer to park in the back, but I didn't want to spend any more time back there than I had to. It was bad enough that whichever office I chose would overlook that exact area, where Stephen had died. I turned on the local NPR station and listened to the Community Calendar. It was ninety percent events happening in Honolulu, and hardly anything in Mahina.

A few minutes later, Pat's vegetable-oil-fueled Mercedes diesel pulled up next to me, wafting a delicious french-fry scent. We exited our respective cars, locked up, and started walking.

"You okay, Molly?" Pat asked.

I nodded.

"Right before I came here, Donnie was telling me, don't stay any longer than you have to, be careful, don't go snooping, and I thought, oh, he's being overprotective as usual."

"No, in this case I can kind of see his point," Pat said. "Come on, I want to show you something."

We walked around the hospital to the old Inebriate Asylum. Surrounding it was untamed jungle. I could hear the roar of a river running through an unseen gorge.

"Look at the top floor," Pat said. "The windows."

"That's where we were yesterday." I shaded my eyes with my hand and tipped my head back to see.

"How many windows do you see on the top floor?" Pat asked.

"Can I count that one that's half hidden behind the tree?" I asked.

"Yeah."

"Four. Why?"

"There are only three rooms on this side on the top floor," Pat said. "311, 312, and 314."

"So one of the offices just has two windows. Hey, thank you for pointing that out. That's the one I want. Let's go have a look. Oh, Serena told me to call security to let us in."

I pulled out my phone.

"I can let us—" Pat began, but I shushed him.

"No B&E today, Pat. I have to do this by the book."

"You're just like Darren on Bewitched," Pat grumbled. "Not letting me use my powers for good."

"Pat, I'm a department chair now. I have to set a good example."

We trudged up the steps and waited. After around ten minutes, a security guard showed up. He was someone I hadn't seen before, and none of his keys worked in any of the locks.

"That's okay," I assured him. "Our department is moving into this floor. I just wanted to have a look around."

Once the guard had left us, Pat asked,

"Do you want me to—"

"Yes, please."

Pat picked the locks and opened the doors to each room in turn: room 310 on our left, and 311, 312, and 314, all of which faced the back of the hospital building.

I thought room 310 might be a good choice, as it was the only one that didn't look out at the back of the hospital. I was hoping it would have a view of the bay, because of its location. But I ruled it out as soon as I opened the door. In size and shape it was the mirror image of the bathroom, with the same narrow footprint, small window, and tiled green floor with a drain in the center. In the center of the room stood a rust-speckled stainless-steel contraption that looked like the offspring of an iron lung and a breadbox.

"No way!" Pat rushed to the device, grasped a handle, and lifted what I suppose you would call the lid. The device opened like an iron maiden. It seemed to be designed for an average-sized human to fit inside.

"What is that?" I hung back in the doorway, half-afraid that Pat was going to try to put me into the thing.

"It's a fever cabinet." Pat had his phone out and was taking pictures of the contraption from every possible angle. "This would have been considered the state-of-the-art medical care before World War 2. I wonder when they got this. Molly, have you heard of Julius Wagner-Jauregg?"

"No. Why? Did someone put him in that gizmo?"

"He won the Nobel Prize in 1927."

"Yay?"

"For his work in pyrotherapy. The use of fever to treat disease. He used malaria to treat late-stage syphilis, which up until then had been a death sentence. He had a soldier with malaria admitted into his ward, and he decided to draw the guy's blood and use it to infect his syphilitic patients."

"How…innovative. Did it work?"

"Yeah. Well. Except for the fifteen percent of patients it killed."

"Ah."

"Oh, and don't be tempted to celebrate him like he was some kind of hero."

"I wasn't going to, but okay."

"He was a member of the Nazi party, he sterilized patients who he thought masturbated too much, and he said working women were degenerate and unable to bear children or breast feed."

"Ha, joke's on him. I'm a working woman and I'm like a walking dairy over here. So what does all this have to do with that human toaster oven or whatever it is?"

"Yeah, sorry for getting off topic. I've been doing a lot of research on early twentieth century medical treatments for this series. It kind of is a human toaster oven. The idea is to give patients the benefit of fever therapy without infecting them with malaria. They'd shut patients into this thing and raise their internal body temperature to up to 107 degrees."

"That can't have been pleasant," I said. "How long did the patients have to stay in there?"

"Four to six hours at a time, for up to twenty sessions."

I shook my head and pushed back from the doorway.

"I don't think I want office number 310," I said. "Let's look at the other ones."

Rooms 311 and 312 each had a square footprint and a large window with a view of the back of the hospital. Room 314 was similar to the other two, but had koa paneling on the wall instead of green paint.

"I think you should take 314," Pat said.

He had been quietly following me as I'd made my inspections.

"I like the wood paneling. But it seems like it's a little narrower than the others. Unless the paneling just makes it look smaller."

Pat took out his phone and pointed it at the far wall. Then he turned 90 degrees and did the same thing.

"You're right, it is narrower," Pat said. "Not from the window to the door, but about six inches wall-to-wall."

"I don't know if the fancy paneling is worth the smaller space." I went over to the window and looked out. It was overcast and raining. The back of the hospital building looked bleaker than ever.

"Good thing I didn't take my top down," I said.

"What?"

"My car."

I rapped on the wood paneling. "Pat, there must be something on the other side of this. There were four windows. But each office only has one, and there are only three offices."

I knocked on the paneling again.

"What does that sound like?" I asked.

"A paneled wall," Pat said.

A rap on the door interrupted us. It was a security guard, a different one from the last one. I hadn't seen him before either. Unlike the previous guard, this one was young, skinny, and officious. Maybe the other one had reported us snooping around.

"Excuse me, Miss," he said. "May I see your identification?"

I did not appreciate this pimply whippersnapper calling me "Miss" as if I were thirteen years old. At my age, the only people who answer to "Miss" are either drag queens or tragic figures in Southern Gothic novels.

"Of course." I pulled my school ID from my wallet. "I'm Molly Barda. Chair of the management department. College of Commerce. My dean, Dan Watanabe, asked me to come here and—"

"How did you get into this office?" he demanded.

"The door was open," Pat said. It was

true—the door *was* open, after Pat picked the lock.

"And who are you, sir?" the guard asked Pat.

"Professor Barda's Feng Shui consultant," Pat said.

"Just a minute," the guard said, and left. A moment later, he was back.

"OK, you check out." He handed my ID back. He seemed to have thawed a bit now that he knew I was legit.

"I was wondering what's on the other side of this wall," I said. "Do you know?"

He shook his head.

"You gotta call Facilities for that, Professor Barda. But in the meantime, we got you down for Room 314. You should be getting a key within a few weeks. Okay, you two have a good day."

"Guess you just picked your office," Pat said.

"Yeah. I'll let Serena know. So she can cross it off her list."

Chapter Thirty-Three

EMMA CALLED me the next morning, just after Donnie had left for work.

"Emma, I had to pick my office without you." I pressed the phone to activate the speaker and hoisted the baby up to rest her head on my shoulder. I had abandoned the idea of spit up rags, opting instead to throw my shirt in the wash and get a new one when necessary.

"Molly," Emma's voice squawked from the phone on the table, "The paper just published Bee's obituary. And guess what they led with. That Bee Corcoran got the system research grant."

"Emma, you can't still be mad about Bee getting the award—"

"I was looking at the rules for the grant," Emma said. "And guess what. In the event the original awardee leaves the campus, turns down the award, or dies, the winning campus may select an alternate project."

"And?"

"And I'm thinking I should get to Gunderson and tell him to switch the award to my project," Emma declared. "Before the money goes somewhere else."

"Emma, no!"

"What do you mean, no?"

"How is that going to look?"

"Who cares how it looks?"

"Emma, if you try to get Bee's grant money, people will think you're the one who pushed Bee out the window. And your motive will be that you wanted her grant."

Emma was quiet for a moment.

"Emma?"

"Yeah, what? I'm still here."

"If they have to award the money to another project at Mahina State, there's a good chance they'll pick yours anyway."

"How do you know?"

"Fine, I don't know, okay? But I do know it's not a good idea to go steaming up to your dean before Bee's murder is even solved and asking him for Bee's grant money. You can see how that wouldn't look good, can't you? Besides, I don't trust your dean. If Betty's daughter was telling the truth, he's conspiring with the prosecutor to frame my husband for murder."

"Molly, I know what I'm doing. You don't have to be so maternalistic."

"Is that a word?"

"Yeah. It's like paternalistic except for ladies. Look, you should be worried about Margaret Adams. That boy she went to Oregon with is probably the one who killed Bee. Bee fired him, ah? How much you wanna bet he got mad an' pushed her out the window? Go worry about Margaret."

"I am worried about Margaret," I said, "I just don't know what I can do about it from here without risking making things worse. Emma, maybe you don't even want that award. Who knows what kind of strings Gunderson attached to it?"

"Ew, like sexual favors?"

"What? I was thinking more along the lines of kickbacks. Maybe Gunderson used Bee's research to get the system's grant money, and then he got her out of the way, so he could get his hands on the money himself?"

"I dunno," Emma said. "Gunderson wouldn't get the funds free and clear. You know grants don't work like that, ah? It's not like Gunderson can just take the money and go spend it all at Ye Olde Elbow Patch Shoppe or wherever he buys his clothes. He's still gotta spend it on legit stuff. Which, depending on how the grant's set up, could be pretty restrictive."

"Yeah, I remember you telling me—"

"Like the grant I have now, ah? Can't spend on meals, lei, manuscript preparation, stipends, books, dues, journal subscriptions, regular lab supplies, computers, printers, printer supplies, nothing. Okay, so back to my idea about sexual favors. What if Gunderson found out Bee's 'secret' and freaked out?"

"Emma, that's horrible. You think

Gunderson killed her just because of who she was?"

"It happens."

"I know it happens. That's why it's horrible."

Francesca squirmed in my arms. I commenced my "baby march" around the living room, a bouncing gait that usually calmed her down.

"Emma, look, let's get your mind off this. Can you come over?"

"You sure? It's a little early for happy hour, but you could talk me into it."

"I wasn't suggesting happy hour. It's nine in the morning. I meant, we haven't had a rating party in a while."

"Oh yeah. Okay, I'll be there in a few. Don't go anywhere."

I rubbed Francesca's fuzzy little head.

"Don't worry. We'll be right here."

Chapter Thirty-Four

A FEW YEARS AGO, some genius in our administration got rid of in-class teaching evaluations in favor of using a certain well-known online professor ratings site. Because anyone can go on the site and leave feedback, Emma, Pat, and I have made sure to curate our online ratings carefully.

Every so often we have what we call a ratings party, where we leave one another reviews on the site. We draw the line at writing our own reviews. For some reason, that feels wrong.

I brewed coffee and opened a bag of stone cookies. They're like biscotti, too hard to eat by themselves, but great dunked in coffee. I called Pat, but his phone went to voice mail. I texted him to tell him what we were doing.

The baby was fed and napping by the time Emma came by, so we were able to start right in.

First, we each logged in and left effusive, five-star ratings for Pat Flanagan's composition class. Pat is a part-time lecturer, who is hired semester by semester to teach one or two or five sections of composition. He can be let go at any time for any reason –or no reason at all. High online ratings give Pat a bit of an edge relative to the rest of the lecturer pool.

After we had finished heaping praise on Pat, Emma and I went on to write reviews for each other. You would think that Emma and I would give each other—that is, ourselves—positive reviews. But that's not what we do. Unlike Pat, both of us have tenure, which means we can only be fired if the administration actually makes an effort to come up with a reason and then do the paperwork.

Because our continued employment

doesn't depend on our constantly convincing the administration of our worth, our main audience is potential students. So we give each other negative reviews to scare the slackers away from our classes.

Im a 3.5+ gpa student going to med school but could barley pass her class

Imposible 2 cheat cos she changes her tests every year. Unfair!

Her coffee mug is filled with the tears of her students.

I was in the middle of typing out a description of Emma's system for crushing the dreams of future doctors, when my phone beeped with a message from Pat.

Sorry can't join you. Filming lava flow. Check out Park's ratings.

"What's that?" Emma asked.

"Pat texted that he can't come because he's down filming the lava, but we should look at Stephen Park's reviews."

Across the table from me, Emma was already tapping on her phone.

"Gross," Emma said. "It's all reviews from Stephen's fan club. All positive. Everyone loved Stephen Park."

I pulled up Stephen's ratings page on my laptop and scrolled down.

"Not a single disappointed customer," I said. "Emma, how much do you want to bet he wrote these himself?"

"Look at the dates, Molly. The most recent ones were posted after he died. Oh, here's a bad one. 'Loves the ladies, the younger the better.'"

"Okay, maybe he didn't write all of them. Oh, come *on*. Someone posted a link to their blog? Someone went to the trouble of blogging about Stephen Park. Have you ever had a student blog about you?"

"Ew, no, and if I caught someone doing that, I'd call the FBI."

"I'm going to see what she wrote," I said.

"Whoa, before you click the link. It might be a phish whatever da kine."

"Oh yeah. Which one is spear phishing and which one is regular phishing?"

"I forget. Just don't click any links is all you gotta remember."

I stared at the review.

Stephen Park's class was one of my most

unique experiences in Hawaii. Read more on my blog.

I picked out key words from the review and searched. Emma came over to sit next to me.

It didn't take long to find the blog. The author was an exchange student. She had been keeping a record of her Hawaii experiences for the benefit of her friends back home. Her latest entry was dated finals week.

The page featured a photo of the lava flow as a header.

"To Stephen, Who Taught Me About Theater And Life," Emma read.

"The word 'and' shouldn't be capitalized," I said.

"He let his students call him by his first name?" Emma asked.

"He insisted on it," I said. "Because he was a bold, unique iconoclast, exactly like all those other edgy cool profs who swear in class and sleep with their favorite students."

I felt Emma turn to look at me.

"Molly, let it go. He's dead. Weren't you

saying you're not supposed to talk stink about the dead?"

"I was not talking stink. To describe is neither to endorse nor to condemn."

Emma leaned into the screen, blocking my view.

"Whoa. Look at this, Molly. 'One of the guys asked him how he got so jacked in such a short time. He said, I'm a guinea pig for a top-secret project. If I tell you about it, I'll have to kill you.'"

"What an original joke." I pulled the laptop toward me so I could see what she was talking about.

"Maybe it really was a secret, though, Molly. Maybe your idea about Bee killing Stephen wasn't so dumb after all."

"Thank you?"

"Think about it. He's hanging around Bee Corcoran, she's doing this muscle research, suddenly he starts growing muscles too? Just like the animals in her lab?"

I lowered the top of my laptop.

"So now you believe me? That Stephen was taking Bee's magic mouse juice?"

"She was working with rats, Molly, not mice. And it's not 'juice', she was using gene—"

"I know, but 'magic mouse juice' is catchy. Don't you think?"

"I don't care if it's catchy. It's wrong."

"So do you think maybe he found some bad side effects, and Bee was afraid he'd tell someone? She killed him before he could kill her career?"

"Hm." Emma rested her chin in her hand and stared at the table. "So who killed Bee then? Or you think with everything else going on in her life it was like the last straw, she regretted what she did and jumped out the window?"

"Or when she got the award, which remember she hadn't asked for, she realized people would be taking a closer look at her work and would find out what she'd been up to. Emma, I just remembered something. Margaret said that her friend told her that Bee's rats would end up in the wrong cages."

"What?"

"That's a problem, right? I mean, that's

not normal, is it, that lab animals would get mixed up?"

"Uh, yeah, it's a problem. I don't do animal research myself, but I know there's all kinds of controls on it. You can't just go switching your animals around. I knew it, Molly. No one could get results like that unless they were faking."

"Well, wait though. She got results with Stephen, didn't she?"

"Maybe, if he really was taking the treatment himself. But what if he wasn't? What if he was just working out to impress Bee? Yeah, I dunno. It seems like too much of a coincidence, doesn't it?"

"Emma, I know it happens, but I don't understand how someone would fake their research results and think they could get away with it. I mean, wouldn't people find out eventually? Personally, I could never pull it off. I send my datasets to anyone who asks, and they can run their own analysis."

"Yeah, but that's assuming your data's good in the first place. If you wanted to, you could invent survey responses, and then enter 'em, yeah?"

"Oh. I guess so. But why would I do that? Even if I didn't care about ethics or integrity or anything like that, it doesn't seem worth the risk."

"Not to us, cause we already got tenure. We can get away with publishing in mediocre journals for the rest of our careers. Oh, and if Bee had investors interested in commercializing her research? More motivation for her to keep it going at all costs. Still too early for booze?" Emma got up and brought our coffee mugs into the kitchen.

"It's only ten in the morning, so yes, still too early," I called into the kitchen. "But I'll take another coffee as long as you're there."

"If Bee was faking her results somehow," Emma said as she returned with two steaming mugs of coffee, "and Stephen knew about it, that's a motive for Stephen's murder that points away from your husband. You should call Honey and tell her."

"I already told her, remember? You were there. Both of you were unimpressed by my theory."

"But you get more evidence now. You found a student's blog about Stephen Park, where he admits to being a guinea pig. Maybe Honey guys can find something else in there that could help Donnie's case."

"You're right," I said. "Worst case, Honey says she's not interested and doesn't want to know about it."

Chapter Thirty-Five

I WAVED to Emma as she drove off, then strapped Francesca into the baby seat in the back of my T-bird. I drove the few blocks down toward the ocean and pulled up to the curb right outside the Drive-Inn. I knew from hard experience that the lane between the Drive-Inn and the recycling center was too narrow for my car.

"Honey wants to talk to you again?" Donnie asked as he lifted Francesca out of her car seat.

"That's what she said."

"Well, if you can remember anything that'll help my case, that would be great. Tell me all about it when you get back." Donnie inserted Francesca into the baby carrier on his chest and grabbed the diaper bag out of the back seat.

"There are two bottles of milk in there," I said. "It shouldn't take long. I should be back in forty-five minutes at most."

"Take as much time as you need." Donnie patted the T-bird's top and turned to go.

I drove down to Honey's office feeling optimistic. But after her first few questions, I wondered why I had even bothered.

No, I didn't have any evidence that Bee had faked her results.

No, I didn't have any witnesses to Bee going out onto the terrace that night, much less pushing Stephen off it.

No, I didn't have any idea who Bee's investor might be, nor any evidence that she even had an investor.

Yes, I could see how Stephen's "but then I'd have to kill you" comment could have been simply a joke.

No, I had no evidence that Stephen Park had been taking any kind of experimental drug or treatment.

Honey had even more bad news for me.

Betty Jackson's daughter was on the mainland visiting relatives and was unavailable for questioning. I didn't blame Betty for sending Verna away. Of course she would protect her daughter. I'd do the same thing in her place. Unfortunately for Donnie (and me), there was no one else who could corroborate Verna's account of the conversation between the dean and the prosecutor.

"Well, Professor," Honey said, standing up and offering a handshake. "I appreciate your keeping me informed. I'll talk it over with my investigator, and it'll be interesting to see what happens when the autopsy comes back."

I went back outside, started the engine, and let it warm up.

Honey's lack of interest was disappointing. Maybe she thought Stephen had been joking, but making something up about being a "guinea pig" wasn't the kind of thing Stephen would do. I considered telling Stephen's parents, but decided against it. I didn't have anything solid for them, and I didn't want to be the one to tell them that their son was using an unproven experimental treatment. It would seem like I was calling Stephen vain and reckless. He *was* vain and reckless, but there was no point in rubbing their noses in it. Maybe I'd get some grocery shopping done and then go back and get the baby from Donnie. Then at least he wouldn't know how humiliatingly short my meeting with Honey had been.

As I shifted into Drive, my phone hummed. I engaged the parking brake again and picked it up.

Emma had sent me a text, so I called her back.

"Molly, you done already?"

"Yes. Unfortunately, I don't think Honey Akiona was very impressed by anything I told her."

"Did you tell her what Stephen said about being a guinea pig?"

"Yes, I did. As I said, she was unimpressed."

"What are you doing right now?"

"Sitting in my car in downtown Mahina

with the engine running. Why? What are you doing?"

"I'm at the old hospital. Meet me on the fourth floor."

"Emma, isn't that where Bee's lab—"

But she had already hung up. Now I was decidedly curious. I shifted into drive and pulled out onto the road.

Chapter Thirty-Six

THE DOOR to Bee Corcoran's lab was ajar, propped open with one of those contentious plastic door stops you can buy in packs of two at the hardware store.

I say "contentious" because those little wedges are at the heart of a conflict between two powerful factions at Mahina State. The Student Retention Office has decreed that we should keep our office doors open at all times in order to be welcoming to students. But Facilities has ordered us to keep our office doors shut to comply with fire regulations. To show they mean business, Facilities conducts random sweeps, confiscating door wedges and locking office doors behind them. Pity the unsuspecting professor who comes back from the bathroom to find herself locked out of her office right before class. Let's just say I've learned the hard way to take my key with me everywhere.

I pushed the door open. Inside Bee's lab, the lights were off. Sunlight filtered through the tall window, which was now crisscrossed with yellow police tape. The rat cages were empty and the water bottles were gone.

"Emma?" I called softly.

"In here, Molly."

Emma had a cardboard box open. She was pulling out beakers and pipettes and other science-y-looking objects and setting them down on the counter.

"What are you doing?" I asked. "You're going to get your fingerprints on everything."

Emma gave me an exasperated look and held up her gloved hands for me to see.

"Grab a pair from that box next to the sink," she said.

I went over, pulled out two purple gloves, and tugged them on.

"What are we looking for?" I asked.

"Notebooks."

"What?"

"Come on, help me out. Where would you hide lab notebooks you needed to get to but didn't want anyone else to find?"

"Are you talking about actual paper notebooks?"

Emma sighed heavily.

"No, plasma notebooks. Yes, paper notebooks, Molly."

"It's the twenty-first century. Who uses paper notebooks anymore?"

"Anyone who works in the field. Or in a wet lab."

"Well, that's charmingly retro," I said.

"Yep, that's why we do it."

"Emma, are you sure this is a good idea? What if someone comes in and sees us rummaging around wearing gloves?"

"Molly, you can stay and help me, or if you're too chicken then you can leave. Just don't stand there kibitzing."

I considered pulling the gloves off and

walking out, but I couldn't do it. My curiosity wouldn't allow me to leave. I went over to the far wall and started opening drawers.

"If she did keep notebooks, how do you know they're even here?" I asked. "What if they're at her house? Or in her car?"

"I keep mine in my lab," Emma said. "So do most people I know. Eh, what happened with the lawyer? How come she didn't care about our new evidence?"

"She said she'd mention it to her investigator." I slid open a drawer. It was empty, except for a sandwich bag full of plastic forks. "The thing is, we don't have any evidence for any of our brilliant theories. A second-hand report of a remark Stephen made to his theater class last semester doesn't count, apparently."

"Did you tell her we were thinking that there must've been an investor who had a stake in her research, then it turned out it didn't work, or it had some serious side effects?"

"If there was a secret formula, I'm pretty

sure it worked. You haven't seen Stephen this summer, have you?"

"Nope."

"When I saw him he was a total 'after' picture. And it was different from all the other times his weight has yo-yoed."

"What about when he went through his exercise addiction phase and was at the gym all the time?" Emma asked.

"That's what I'm talking about. All he did was walk on the treadmill for hours, and he was emaciated then. I've only ever seen him scrawny or fat. The night he died was the only time I've ever seen him look muscular. Do you hear something?"

We both fell silent as footsteps echoed down the hallway outside. Emma ran to the door and peered out. Then she waved at me frantically.

"Act natural," she ordered, shoving me out into the hallway. She followed me out and pulled the door shut behind her.

"Hands in your pockets," she whispered. "Walk with me toward the exit sign."

"What? I don't have pockets."

I saw Geoffrey Gunderson walking

toward us and quickly clasped my purple-gloved hands behind my back.

"Oh, hi Geoffrey," Emma said casually as we passed him in the hallway. "Hey, how's your summer going?"

Geoffrey Gunderson stopped walking, which meant we had to stop too.

"I've certainly had better, I must say. My goodness, just when you think one crisis has passed...and what brings you ladies in on this fine day?"

"Fine day?" I wondered whether Gunderson had been outside at all. It was overcast, drizzly, and steaming hot.

"Uh, Molly was just showing me the new College of Commerce offices," Emma said.

Geoffrey Gunderson gave me an odd look.

"Here in this building? Did Dan tell you he had space in the old hospital? I was given to understand that the College of Commerce offices were in the next building over."

"No, you're right," I said. "Dan did tell me that the College of Commerce has the building out back. We're here to look around. I was just reading about this building. How it was constructed in in the style of an Italian Renaissance palace."

I'd started reading *Island Confidential* again. Pat's latest installment of Mysterious Mahina had a history of the old Mahina Memorial building.

"Ahem. Well," Gunderson started over. "We're certainly fortunate to have such beautiful surroundings. And to rescue this wonderful historic building from the elements and the termites. Such a lovely opportunity. Although the termites can be so destructive, so, so destructive..."

The dean's gaze flicked briefly to a point behind us, roughly where Bee's lab was.

"Well, it was nice to see you, Geoffrey," Emma said. "Okay, Molly, back to your office, ah?"

As soon as we were in the stairwell I rolled the gloves off my hands. I was about to put them in my purse when I realized something.

"My purse is in Bee's lab," I said.

"You need it right now?" Emma asked.

"This minute? While Gunderson's prowling around?"

"Well…"

"We can come back and get it later when we're sure he's gone."

"Okay. My phone's in there too. Can I borrow yours? I need to text Donnie and tell him I might be a little bit later than I planned."

Chapter Thirty-Seven

"I FINALLY GET to see your new office," Emma said, as I struggled to the top floor of the Inebriates Asylum building. "Molly, you okay?"

I held up my finger and she waited for me to catch my breath.

"That was unfortunate timing," I panted. "Your dean showing up. Geez, I hope I get used to these stairs soon. I feel like my heart's going to explode."

It had started to rain. The frosted skylight glowed silver, casting a sickly glow over the landing.

"Taking this many stairs is tough if you're not used to it." Emma went over to the railing and looked down. "You could take the elevator if you weren't so scared of it."

"I don't know. It's the old cage kind, and you know how things are maintained here—"

"Eh, Molly, how many ghosts you think are hanging around here? I bet there's a bunch of 'em watching us right now, ah?"

I stood with my back pressed against the door of office 311, watching Emma lean over the railing.

"If the dead really are watching us, Emma, they're probably asking themselves why you seem so eager to join them."

"What are you talking about?"

"Considering two people have just fallen to their deaths, why are you leaning on the railing like that?"

"That was the next building over," Emma retorted.

"Did you hear what Gunderson said about termites? You should get away from there."

"Fine. We can kill some time in your office, then go back and get your purse when we know Gunderson's gone. Does that work?" Emma finally turned away from the terrifying railing.

"Sure. Dang it. I should've pumped before I came here. Or brought my breast pump." I crossed my arms over my chest, feeling the familiar heaviness.

"Aw, why I gotta hear about that?" Emma complained. "Come on, show me your new office."

I tried the handle of 314, but it was locked.

"They never gave you the key?" Emma asked.

"Serena says it's going to take a while. They're going to wait until everyone's picked their office, and issue all of the new faculty keys at once."

"You gotta wait until Hanson Harrison gets back from Martha's Vineyard or wherever he goes all summer?" Emma asked. "Doesn't he always get back after class starts, with some story about how he missed his connection in Boston?"

"Yup. So I expect to get my key sometime around the middle of fall semester. I guess I'll have to call security to let us in. Can I use your phone again?"

"Nah, that'll take forever. Come on, move over."

Emma pulled something out of her jeans pocket and hunched over the door handle.

"You know how to pick locks?" I exclaimed as the door swung open.

"Pat showed me. You should learn."

"Ow," I crossed my arms tightly as I followed her in. "I really should've brought my pump with me. What was I thinking, leaving it in the diaper bag? It's not like Donnie can use it."

"I'm not listening," Emma declared. "Eh, this is nice. It's like the other one except you got koa on the wall. Bet you this office belonged to an administrator, ah? All deluxe."

She rapped on the paneling.

"Aren't you a biology professor?" I asked. "How are you squeamish about breastfeeding?"

"There's a reason I study plants, Molly. Eh, speaking of termites. I think you got 'em in the wall here."

"What? Where? How can you tell?"

"See how this gives, right here?" Emma pressed on the paneling.

As she spoke, an entire section of the wall gave way and swung open like a door.

Chapter Thirty-Eight

BEFORE US LAY A SQUARE ROOM, a mirror image of the one we were standing in. The only light source was the dusty window, shaded by the branches of a mango tree outside.

"The fourth window," I exclaimed.

"What fourth window?" Emma asked.

"From the outside you see four windows, but from the inside there are only three doors on this wall. Pat showed me. I forgot about it until now."

"Aw, that's cool." Emma strode into the little room, and I cautiously followed her.

The room smelled close and mildewed. I

went over to the casement window and tried to open it.

"Having trouble?" Emma asked.

"It's stuck," I said.

Emma came over and muscled it open, releasing a cascade of paint flakes.

"How do you do that?" I asked.

"Canoe paddling, Molly. You could still join us for practice. It's not too late."

"Thanks again, and again, no thank you."

"Look at this, though, you got a secret room. How cool is this?"

The room was furnished with a simple bookshelf, a faded horsehair chair that used to have a floral pattern, and a small side table. Behind the table was a ghostly gray smudge on the wall.

"There's no lamp here. Or outlets." I looked up at the ceiling; there was no light fixture.

"And there's no exit door," I said. "Let's make sure this thing doesn't slam shut."

I pushed the door all the way open and then pulled the side table over to brace it.

"Molly," Emma said from the window, "you got a good view here. It's the end window so you see part of the hospital, but a lot of your view is trees. What do you think this room was for?"

"I don't know. There's not a lot here to go on, is there?"

I opened the drawer of the table in hopes of discovering some ancient hidden treasure, but it looked empty. Unthinkingly, I slid my hand to the back of the drawer. My fingers landed on something cold and metallic.

"Emma, look. What is this thing?"

Emma turned away from the window to squint at the object I was holding up. It looked like a fancy little trowel. It was adorned with scrolls and curlicues and coated in black tarnish.

"I dunno. Probably some torture device for the mentally ill. You should leave it here, Molly."

Out of some kind of rebellious impulse, I slipped the item into my bra.

"You're probably right," I said. "Okay, I think I need to get home. Are you ready to go?"

"Sure." Emma pushed the window shut as the rain started to pour down in earnest. We went back out the way we came in, closed everything behind us, and finally made sure the door to Room 314 was locked.

"Well, that was exciting," I said.

"Yeah, you got a double-wide office."

"Sounds extra classy when you put it that way."

"Let's try stop by Bee's lab," Emma said. "Gunderson's gotta be gone by now."

"I hope so. I'm swelling up like a prizewinning pumpkin. *Two* prizewinning pumpkins, if you want to be precise about it."

"Maybe we can find that notebook—" Emma caught a glimpse of my anguished expression and changed course. "Tell you what. You get your purse and go. I'll stick around and keep looking."

"I don't think that's a good idea," I said. "You shouldn't be there alone. Even if there's no murderer hanging around, what if a shelf falls on you or the floor gives way or something? The railing already gave way.

If you're here by yourself, you won't be able to call for help."

Going downstairs took much less effort than going up. Going down I was able to listen to what Emma was saying when I wasn't gasping for breath.

"I don't wanna wait too long," Emma said. "I'm worried Facilities is gonna get their orders to clean out the lab, and they'll sweep everything out and dump it in the landfill. I wanna see if I can find Bee's notebooks before that happens. Tell you what, I'll take a super quick look around one last time, and then we can leave together. It'll only take a second."

"Fine," I said, hugging myself tightly. "But we really do have to be quick."

Chapter Thirty-Nine

EMMA and I took the side stairwell back up to Bee's lab. Emma had to keep stopping to wait for me because, frankly, I was a wreck. My legs were jelly, my chest felt like two bursting water balloons, and I was so hungry I felt like I was going to black out.

"I should buy a pedometer," I gasped, as we reached the fourth floor for the second time that afternoon.

"They don't make you any faster," Emma said, breezing ahead of me.

"I know that," I wheezed as I struggled to keep up with her. "I just want a quantitative measurement of my suffering."

Bee's lab looked the same as we'd left it

earlier, filled with appliances that looked like bizarro versions of things you'd find in your kitchen. The autoclave was basically a desktop dishwasher. The incubator looked like a refrigerator, but when you opened it, it was warm inside, not cold. A fume hood served the same purpose as the hood over your stove, but it was huge, with a sealed-off workspace underneath.

The lab was close and stuffy, and I felt myself start to sweat. I spotted my purse sitting next to the sink and slung it onto my shoulder before I had the chance to forget it again. The box of gloves was right there, so I pulled on another pair.

"Okay, real quick," Emma said. "We're looking for anything that looks like a notebook. Open every drawer and cabinet. Think about where you'd put a notebook."

"I keep everything backed up online," I said.

"Just look, Molly. The sooner you find something, the sooner we can go."

"We have to find something?" I objected. "I thought you said it would just be a second."

"Molly, weren't you just on my case for standing too close to the railing? Get away from there and help me look, ah? Oh, I gotta take a bio break. Don't go anywhere. I'll be right back."

I realized I was standing next to the window. Two strips of yellow tape printed with the word CAUTION formed an X over the closed blinds.

I shuddered, backed away slowly, and banged my lower back on something. It was the corner of a long narrow counter that bisected the room.

The counter had a single shallow drawer at its end. You wouldn't see it unless you were standing by the window. I pulled it open. The drawer contained three boxes of purple nitrile gloves: Small, medium, and large. Something made me pick up the small box.

Underneath was a black-and-white composition notebook.

I picked the notebook up. National brand. *That's a strangely generic name*, I thought.

"Emma?" I called out, but remembered she'd gone to the bathroom.

"I'll take that," said a man's voice from the doorway.

Dean Geoffrey Gunderson strode in, holding out his hand.

He was coming right at me. From Gunderson to me to the open window was almost a straight line. All he needed to do was pick up a little speed. The blinds were closed, but they weren't much of a barrier.

This is what happened to Bee, I thought.

"Emma!" I yelled, as the weedy medievalist picked up speed.

Force equals mass times acceleration.

Why was my brain feeding me formulas from freshman physics, of all things? Gunderson didn't have a lot of mass, but he did seem to be coming at me pretty fast.

Momentum equals mass times velocity.

"She was keeping two sets of books," I blurted out.

"That is not your property, Professor Barda. Please give it to me."

Gunderson kept coming closer.

"If this comes out..." I started, then

trailed off. What would be the point of running my mouth? It would just make him want to kill me even more.

Geoffrey Gunderson closed the distance between us and reached his arm toward me. I considered darting around him, but I was blocked by a wall and a file cabinet.

"Emma. *Emma!*"

My chest ached. All I wanted was to be home with Donnie and baby Francesca. Curiosity killed the professor. Why had I agreed to look for the notebook? Where was Emma? I had to think fast.

And then it came to me.

I dropped the notebook at my feet. With my right hand, I pulled my shirt and bra up with a single, well-practiced gesture. With my left hand I pressed my engorged breast.

A needle-thin jet of milk drummed against Gunderson's glasses, temporarily blinding him. As he clawed at his eyes, I saw Emma climbing up on the counter behind him. She looked around, picked up a large glass flask, raised it up, and brought it down hard.

"Ouch!" he cried, and rubbed his head. Which was not what we were expecting.

But Emma was not out of ideas. She snatched Gunderson's milk-splashed glasses.

"I'm calling the police," she declared, holding the glasses over her head.

"Yes, please do." Gunderson pulled a handkerchief from the inside of his suit jacket and dabbed his eyes.

"And don't you go anywhere," she warned.

"I don't suppose I can," he said in her general direction, "until such time as my spectacles are returned to me."

Emma stood on the counter and made the call while I put myself back together. We waited in uncomfortable silence until Detective Medeiros showed up.

Chapter Forty

IF MY FAIRY godmother came to me and granted me the power to erase only one memory, I would probably pick that afternoon's interview at Mahina Police Department Headquarters.

Detective Medeiros herded us all into a single room with a small table at its center. I had always thought that witnesses were questioned one by one, but maybe Medeiros thought he could save some time with the focus group approach. He sat me, Emma, and Geoffrey Gunderson on one side of a scarred wooden table, and himself on the other.

"I'd like someone to tell me what's going

on," Medeiros said. "Two people have died in that building, and now three Mahina State University professors are getting into a brawl and calling the police on each other."

"It was self-defense," Emma said. I nodded.

"These women were stealing university property," Gunderson countered.

"He's just saying that cause he killed Bee Corcoran," Emma retorted.

Gunderson turned to stare at Emma. If he had been wearing a monocle, it would have dropped into his lap.

"Emma!" he gasped. "Are you saying I killed Bee? How can you even think such a thing?"

"Why would he do that?" Medeiros asked patiently.

"Maybe he killed her because he found out her research results were fake," Emma said, "and he was afraid when it got out it would ruin his reputation. Cause he's the one who got her the system life sciences award."

"You say her results were fake?"

Medeiros wrote on his tiny notebook and looked up at Emma. "Do you have evidence of this?"

"Detective," Gunderson pleaded, "From what I know of these two ladies, they are good, kind people at heart. But they appear to be in the grip of a *folie a deux*. I can think of no other explanation for this fanciful slander, to say nothing of the…"

Gunderson turned to stare at me.

"… assault upon my person!"

"Assault, ah?" Medeiros wrote in his notebook. "And how, precisely, did Dr. Nakamura assault you, Dr. Gunderson?"

"Me!" Emma exclaimed.

"Oh, no, it wasn't Emma. It was Molly here. I caught her taking property from the lab and asked her to hand it to me. And she…ahem."

Medeiros looked at me in a sort of appraising way, and then at Gunderson, and then back at me. As if he were struggling to reconcile the accusation of physical assault with the pencil-necked weaklings sitting in front of him.

"Well. You know she's from the *business*

school," Gunderson added gratuitously, as if that were sufficient to explain my antisocial behavior.

"I was acting in self-defense," I said. "I thought he was going to push me through the window. He was coming straight at me. And I thought when it was happening that that's what probably happened to Bee Corcoran."

"And what did Professor Barda do to you, Dr. Gunderson, that you would characterize as assault?"

"Well, she… she …er…the truth is, I didn't quite see everything that happened. *She* knows what she did."

All eyes turned to me.

"Would you like to explain, Professor Barda?" Detective Medeiros asked.

I flashed back to the sight of Gunderson's eyes widening with astonishment, just before the jet of milk blasted his bifocals like a hose turned on a window…

"No, Detective, I would prefer not to explain, if it's all the same to you."

Then I realized I had a way to change the subject.

"I know about the conversation at the Maritime Club," I blurted out. "About pinning the blame for Stephen's murder on my husband. Geoffrey Gunderson was there."

"With all due respect," Gunderson said, "you have no idea what you're talking about."

Gunderson's words were confident, but I could sense a rise in his anxiety level. I might have been picking up a subtle odor of flop sweat.

"Professor Barda?" Medeiros prompted. "Let's stick to the subject. Why does Professor Gunderson say you assaulted him?"

"I didn't touch him," I said.

"Well if you won't tell 'em, I will." Emma then provided an unnecessarily-detailed account of the incident, which I see no need to reproduce here. As she elaborated on her story, piling on the prurient details, Medeiros put the heels of his hands over his eyes. Just the way I do when I get those stabbing pains on the side of my head.

"Okay, now we got that out of the way," Emma declared, with the brisk air of someone dusting off her hands. "Molly, tell 'em about the conversation at the Maritime Club."

"Yes, why don't you do that?" Medeiros set his pad down and leaned back in his chair.

I had to proceed carefully. I knew prosecutors worked closely with the police. Accusing Pang outright might be risky. I would tell the story, but leave the prosecutor's name out.

"Stephen Park died after a fall at the donor dinner," I said.

Medeiros nodded.

"He went out onto a lanai area adjacent to the dining room. There were no barricades or signs saying to keep off."

"It was a donor dinner," Gunderson interrupted. "We couldn't exactly put out orange traffic cones and flashing warning signs."

"Not even if it could have saved someone's life?" I said self-righteously.

Gunderson gave an indignant little sniff.

"The area was poorly lit, and the railing was too low to be safe," I continued, as Medeiros scribbled in his tiny notebook. "Stephen's parents are suing the university because they believe those unsafe conditions led to their son's death. But Dr. Gunderson tried to steer the investigation so that Stephen's death would be blamed on something or someone besides the university. My husband, Donnie Gonsalves, made a convenient scapegoat because years ago I was romantically involved with Stephen Park. Accusing my husband seemed like the path of least resistance. If Stephen was killed by a jealous husband, that would reduce the university's exposure."

"Why that's—" Gunderson sputtered.

"Professor Barda," Medeiros cut him off. "Do you have any evidence of this conspiracy to obstruct justice? Because that's what it sounds like."

"Yes. At a recent event at the Maritime

Club, Dr. Gunderson was overheard in conversation with...another party, discussing pinning the blame on Donnie. My husband."

"Who was the other party?'" Medeiros asked, going directly to the question that I was hoping not to have to answer.

"I believe it was someone from the prosecutor's office," I said.

"Is it true, Dr. Gunderson?" Medeiros asked.

"Er," he said. He looked pale, and his fingers twitched. "Detective, might we continue our discussion in private?"

Medeiros looked at each one of us in turn.

"This is simply an informal interview," he said, finally. "You're free to go at any time."

Emma and I got up so fast we practically knocked our chairs over.

"You know the way out," Medeiros added.

"Molly will forward you the recording," Emma called back to Medeiros as we exited into the fluorescent-lit hallway.

"Recording? Of wha...yes, the recording," I repeated.

"Why did you tell him there was a recording?" I whispered as we hurried down the hallway toward the exit sign.

"Nah, it was good. It's gonna keep Gunderson honest if he thinks there's a recording."

We emerged from the police station into the hazy afternoon. Steam curled up from the puddles in the parking lot. I felt my bag vibrate, and pulled out my phone.

"Ooh," I said. "I have a few messages from Honey Akiona. She wants me to come to her office right away. Darn it, I was hoping to go home finally."

We approached our cars. Emma's unlocked with a chirp when she rested her hand on the door handle.

"At least you figured out a way to get rid of your milk," she said as she climbed into the driver's seat.

"Emma," I said. "We will never speak of this again."

"Maybe *you* won't." She pulled the door

shut, backed out of her space, and zoomed off.

I drove back to Honey Akiona's office, wondering what she wanted. She couldn't possibly know what had just happened.

Except that she did know. She had a police scanner, and friends in Mahina PD. She debriefed me, followed up with some pointed questions, and explained (at length) the importance of leaving crime investigations to the professionals.

After I swore to her never, ever, to interfere with any investigation ever again, Honey rewarded me with a morsel of good news about Donnie's case.

I drove home feeling chastened but encouraged. Despite everything that had gone wrong that day, at least one thing had gone right. Bee Corcoran's lab notebook was tucked under the floormat of my Thunderbird.

Chapter Forty-One

"HOW DID IT GO WITH HONEY?" Donnie asked, when we'd gotten seated at the kitchen counter. I knew it wasn't right to keep secrets from my husband (to say nothing of the general futility of trying to keep anything secret in Mahina). I tried to think of the best way to present the day's news. Positive first, I decided. Then I could hit him with the visit to Bee's lab and the subsequent trip to the police station. There wasn't going to be a better time. The baby was fed, and we were about to dig in to plates of tasty Drive-Inn leftovers. Tonight it was Spam fried rice, chicken katsu, and potato mac salad.

"The good news is, Honey says they're having trouble building a case against you," I said. "She thinks Pang might give up soon if they can't get anything solid. Yes, he wants to bank a favor with the university, but he doesn't want it so badly that he's willing to do something risky like plant evidence or bribe witnesses. Also, you contributed to his campaign, so Honey thinks that helps a little."

"Maybe not," Donnie said grimly. "If he wants to make a show of being tough and principled, what better way than to bite the hand of one of your donors?"

"Well. That's my good news, anyway."

Donnie dug into his potato mac salad. "Hm. A little heavy on the mustard. What do you think?"

"Do you want to hear the rest of my news, or not?"

"I don't know. Is it good?"

I wrinkled my nose and shrugged. I was proud that I'd managed to secure Bee Corcoran's notebook, even if I couldn't decipher anything inside it except her initials. And I was looking forward to going over it with Emma tomorrow. But I doubted Donnie would feel as positive about it as I did. He'd probably just focus on the fact that I'd stolen something that belonged to a possible murder victim.

"So…how bad is it?" He asked carefully.

"I wouldn't say bad exactly. Emma and I had kind of a little adventure today, that's all. Everyone's okay, and no harm done. Know what?" I stood up. "Before we get into all that, why don't I get us some wine?"

Chapter Forty-Two

DONNIE DIDN'T SCOLD ME, or yell at me, or even scowl at me. Instead, as I told him about the events of that afternoon, he sat very still. By the time I got to part where I was being interviewed by Detective Medeiros, I realized I'd been doing all the talking. But I could tell Donnie had heard me, if only because of his white knuckles and thousand-yard stare.

When I finished he nodded, stood up, and without looking at me or saying a word, walked down the hallway and went to bed.

Things were almost back to normal the next morning. Before he left for work,

Donnie hugged me extra-hard, begged me to stay safe, and hugged me again. Then he offered to take the baby to work with him, so that I could get some rest. I assured him that the baby would be safe with me. He seemed skeptical. When he left, he promised to check in on us as soon as he could.

I didn't tell Donnie this, but I was practically dancing with anticipation. Emma was going to come over and decipher the contents of Bee's mysterious lab notebook.

Unfortunately, it wasn't a matter of Emma walking in, cracking the book open, and instantly solving the mystery. The book was about three-quarters filled with handwriting that looked more like an inky scribble than like actual words. Emma sat at the dining table near the window to get the best natural light. She went over each page slowly, often flipping back a few pages. (This was very frustrating to me.) Frequently she would go to her phone to look something up.

Meanwhile, I walked the baby, brought Emma coffee, nursed the baby, drank about a gallon of water, refilled Emma's coffee, set out crackers, cheese, and chocolates, ate most of it, changed the baby, emptied the diaper holder, refilled Emma's coffee again, got the baby to sleep, and brewed more coffee.

"Anything?" I would ask Emma every so often.

She would shake her head as if shaking off an annoying bug.

Then, after an entire morning of this, Emma cried, "Oh!"

I came running over to the kitchen counter, holding Francesca. Francesca was wide awake at this point and in the mood to grab things. She reached for Emma's hair and I pulled her out of range just in time.

"Hang on," Emma stalled me again, "Let me just make sure."

She continued to turn pages, muttering phrases like "milligrams per kilogram" and "tissue fibrosis" and something that sounded like "Sea Terminus."

Finally, she snapped the notebook shut.

"Okay," she said. "I figured it out."

"The murders?" I asked excitedly.

"How she got her *results*," Emma retorted, as if I should know that that was far more important. "I knew she was cooking the books. But now I know how she was doing it."

"Okay," I said, doing my best to hide my disappointment. "What does this have to do with her murder?"

"Molly. You wanna know what I found, or no?"

"Sure." I put Francesca into her playpen, sat down next to Emma, and feigned interest. "How was Bee cooking the books?"

"Okay, let's review. There's a thing our body makes that keeps our muscles from growing too big or too fast. Bee was trying to figure out a way to counteract it. And so are a bunch of other researchers around the world."

"I remember. Yeah, I probably have a double dose of it, whatever it is," I said. "I can't build muscle no matter what I do."

"You never know until you try, Molly."

"What do you mean? I have tried. Don't you remember, you talked me into signing up for that—"

"You wanna hear what I found or not?" Emma demanded.

"Sure."

"Okay. I'll make it real simple for you. She set up three groups of rats. One group, she just let them live their rat lives. She didn't give 'em drugs or nothing. That's what we call the control group."

"Thank you, Emma, I know what a control group is."

"The second group of rats got steroids, you know about those, yeah?"

"Yes."

"And the third group got the treatment that's supposed to suppress this muscle-limiting thing."

"I'm with you. Three groups of rats. Control group, standard no-big-deal treatment, fancy new Bee Corcoran treatment. So what happened?"

"They inflicted an injury and then saw how fast the muscle recovered."

"Oh no, poor rats."

"Yeah, like I said, I'm glad I work with plants. Anyway, the experimental group, the one with Bee's treatment? Had worse muscle recovery. And some of them died."

"Did more die in Bee's treatment group than in the other groups?" I asked.

"Yeah."

"Wow. That's bad. So the obvious question is, how did she end up winning the system research grant?"

Emma started to open the notebook and then shut it again.

"It's kinda complicated. I'll give you the English major version."

"Fine. Give me the English-major version."

"Okay. When a rat from her treatment group started dragging, she'd switch it with a rat from one of the other two groups. Then when it died, the death would be counted as one of the control group or the steroid group. Do that with enough rats and it looks like the treatment is just as safe as the other two conditions."

"She was switching the rats," I exclaimed. "Margaret's friend was right. Except Bee wasn't careless, she was doing it on purpose."

"Heck yeah, she was doing it on purpose. What about Margaret's friend?"

"The young man we saw in Bee's lab, who told us it was his last day on the job. That's why she fired him. Because he figured out that she was switching the rats around. Except he just thought she was being careless. Remember, I asked you whether you wanted to hire him, and you said no?"

"I did?"

"Yes. You said you didn't want some kid coming in and telling you how to run your lab."

"I don't remember that at all. Molly, your memory must be going."

"So when Stephen Park talked about being someone's guinea pig?" I asked. "Do you think he was developing some kind of side effect of the treatment?"

"Maybe."

"Like what?"

Emma leafed through the notebook.

"A lot of the rats died from fibrosis."

"What's fibrosis?"

"Like out of control scar tissue. But here's the thing, humans aren't rats."

"Yeah, *some* humans."

"You know what I mean."

"I'm calling Detective Medeiros," I scooted my chair back and stood up. "If Stephen knew about the treatment's failure, and was ready to blow the whistle, then Dean Gunderson would have a reason to kill them both to cover it up."

"And how you gonna explain to Medeiros how you got the notebook?"

I sat back down.

"Good point. Oh, how about if we send it to Honey Akiona? Anonymously, of course—"

A wet blast noise from the direction of the playpen interrupted me. I retrieved Francesca.

"I'll call her after I change the baby." I rushed down the hallway, holding the baby at arm's length.

"I'll call Honey," Emma shouted after me. "You go do your hazmat cleanup."

"Thank you," I called back. "You can explain it better than I can anyway."

I came back into the living room with the cleaned-up baby, to find Emma pouring herself a glass of vodka. Her phone was lying on the counter next to her glass.

"I told Honey about the rats," Emma said. "She wants to talk to you."

She handed me the phone and took the baby. With her free hand she picked up her glass and started drinking.

"Good news," Honey said. "Donnie's alibi for the time of Bee Corcoran's death holds up. Several regular customers and employees say he was there at Donnie's Drive-Inn."

"That is good news," I said. "Thank you."

Emma set her glass down and gave me a thumbs-up.

"The other thing you should know is that Geoffrey Gunderson also has an alibi for that time. He was in a meeting in Honolulu."

"So Gunderson couldn't have killed Bee," I said.

"That's correct."

"Well then what was he doing snooping around her lab?"

"He says he was in Dr. Corcoran's lab to look it over before Facilities came in. They're going to have to fix that busted railing before anyone else can occupy the space."

"So we're no further along than where we were before," I said.

"Well, I was just talking to Professor Nakamura. And I'll tell you what I said to her. I'll take a look at any information that comes my way. Regardless of where it comes from."

"Thank you," I exclaimed.

"No guarantees, though."

Emma handed me the baby as soon as I disconnected the call.

"I'll run the notebook down to her," she said. "Don't go anywhere."

Chapter Forty-Three

EMMA WAS BACK within half an hour, and Honey called soon after that.

"Medeiros guys have the notebook now," Honey said.

"Fantastic," I said. "That was fast. How did you...never mind. Hang on, Emma's here, so I'm going to put you on speaker. So what happens now?"

"They're gonna get an expert to look at it."

"They should hire me to do it," Emma called from the kitchen.

"Nah, all due respect, tell Professor Nakamura they got their own people."

"It was worth a try," Emma said.

The microwave beeped, and Emma came back into the dining room holding a plate of Drive-Inn leftovers.

"So with Donnie and Dean Gunderson both having alibis," I asked, "who do they think killed Bee?"

"They're probably gonna put it down as suicide," Honey said.

"Oh yeah," Emma cried through a mouthful of Korean chicken. "Cause da kine, ah?"

"Because that's their go-to when they don't have a suspect," Honey said. "What's da kine?"

"Oh, right," I said. "You know, being in the closet?"

"In the closet about what?" Honey asked.

Emma and I looked at each other.

"About being trans," I said.

"Sorry Professor Barda, about what?"

"You know, transgender?" I said. "Identifies as female but was assigned male at birth?"

I thought the phone had gone dead. But then Honey said,

"You're talking about Bee Corcoran?"

"Yes," I said. "She wasn't out about it. And she could pass pretty well. I only know for sure because Stephen told me."

"Stephen Park told you this?"

"I know he shouldn't have. It wasn't his story to tell. But I never told anyone else. Well, not while she was alive. Except Donnie, but that doesn't really count because—"

"Let's go back for a minute," Honey interrupted me. "What exactly did Stephen Park tell you about Bee Corcoran?"

"Well, let's see. He talked about how brave she was to live her truth, how her family wasn't speaking to her, how despite everything she was the most feminine woman he'd ever met, I don't know, I can't remember everything. Basically how awesome and courageous she was. In contrast to me, of course, because according to him I abandoned my true calling and sold out to the business school. That was a favorite theme of his, in fact—"

"Did he ever tell you straight up that Bee Corcoran was transgender?"

"Well, he—"

"Or that she was assigned male at birth?"

"I mean, I don't think he ever phrased it as clinically as that, but he got the message across. That's why her family cut off contact with her. Isn't it?"

"Bee Corcoran was an only child," Honey said. "Her parents passed away years ago. That's why she's not in touch with her family."

"Are you sure about that? Because Stephen—"

"Professor Barda, Bee Corcoran was, how do I put it? She was on her time of month when she died."

"Wow," I said. "They can do that now?"

"No. They can't."

"What do you mean?"

"Stephen Park misled you, Professor. Bee Corcoran was not transgender."

"What? But then why would Stephen... ugh, never mind, I think I just answered my own question."

When I hung up, I noticed that Emma was trying not to laugh.

"I'm glad you think it's funny," I fumed. "I feel like an idiot."

"Sorry, I'm not laughing at you." Emma got up and went into the kitchen. "Well, I kind of am. But it's just such classic Stephen Park. He lets everyone assume he's half-Korean cause his last name is Park, he lets you assume Bee's transgender, cause she's ripped. Eh, at least you never told Stephen's parents, right?"

"I guess. But of all the lies he could have told, why would he choose that one? Why would he try to make me think Bee was trans? It was like he wanted to convince me she had something I didn't. I mean, not like *that*, but it was like he was trying to tell me Bee's backstory was more interesting than mine. Why? What was the point?"

Emma came back out with a bottle of wine and two clean coffee mugs.

"Once again, you just answered your own question. Too early for wine?"

"Nope. Pour away. I can't believe it. What a jerk—"

"Whoa, what about speaking ill of the dead?" Emma slid one arm of the corkscrew under the foil and popped it off in one piece.

"I'm not speaking ill, I'm telling the truth. He's a jerk. It's an objective fact. You know, you're right. I shouldn't be surprised. Stephen is just a big phony. It's not any more complicated than that."

"*Was* a big phony."

"Do you know when he met me, he was going through a Bernardo Bertolucci phase? I'm starting to think that's the only reason we even got together."

"Sorry, I don't know who that is. Bernardo who?"

"A famous Italian director. Well, famous with people who care about that kind of thing, anyway. You know, now that I look back on it, I think the only reason he pursued me is because one, he thought I was Italian and two, I supposedly looked like that actress whose name I keep forgetting. Bee was just another prop for him. To show everyone how adventurous or progressive he was or whatever point he was trying to make. And he tricked me into being *nice* to her."

Emma rocked the cork out of the bottle.

"Tricked you? How'd he do that?"

"I thought she was marginalized because of her gender identity and you're not supposed to be a jerk to marginalized people. If I'd known she was just some fit blonde cis woman I'd have told her to eff right off with her stupid fitness advice. Come on, I'm letting my two-month-old get lazy by carrying her?"

"Molly," Emma whispered. "Let it go. They're both dead."

"*Good!*"

I immediately clapped my hand over my mouth.

"I didn't mean it," I whimpered.

"It's okay, bubbeleh." Emma filled a mug with wine and handed it to me. "We all grieve in our own way."

Chapter Forty-Four

I CAME HOME from a well-baby checkup the following afternoon, to what I thought was an empty house. I put the sleeping baby down in her crib and started to undress for a shower. The sound of voices outside stopped me. I got dressed again, grabbed the baby monitor, and tiptoed down the hallway. The voices were coming from the back lanai.

I recognized one of the voices as Donnie's. Relieved, I went out to the back to see who he was talking to.

The other man was Detective Medeiros.

Both men stood when I came out back. Because there were only two chairs and three people, no one made the first move to sit back down.

"Professor," Medeiros greeted me.

"Where's Francesca?" Donnie asked.

"Sleeping." I held up the baby monitor to show him. "So what's going on?"

"Good news," Donnie said.

"Autopsy results came back," Medeiros said. "Stephen Park died of natural causes."

"Fibrosis?" I guessed, remembering what Emma had told me about the rat research.

"What?" Donnie asked.

"It's an overgrowth of scar tissue, and apparently it can be fatal...sorry. What were the natural causes?"

"The cause of death was abdominal aortic rupture," Medeiros said.

"Oh. What?"

"Since you seem to be interested in the details, the aorta is the main artery of the body, going from the heart down into the abdomen. It can spontaneously rupture, or break—"

"No, no," I interrupted him. "That's okay. Don't describe it. Stephen Park died of a medical condition, though, is what you're saying. Right?"

"Yes."

"He wasn't murdered?"

"No."

"Wow. Okay, so I was wondering, Sorry Donnie, but I have to ask. Detective, Stephen called my name that night as I was walking past. I ignored him. And I kind of assumed he tried again and leaned over too far and fell. I was wondering whether it was my fault he died."

"You were?" Donnie asked.

"Yeah. I was. I've kind of been obsessing about it, to be honest. Thinking, if I'd just stopped and acknowledged him, maybe he'd still be alive, and you wouldn't have had to go through this whole trumped-up...this whole ordeal. But it had nothing to do with me. Is that what you're saying, Detective?"

"Correct. Park's death wasn't caused by anything you did." Medeiros was staring out over the back hedge. Unlike me, he was tall enough to see the graveyard beyond it. "There's nothing you could have done besides call for help, which you did. He was gone before he hit the ground."

"So why do you think he called out to me?" I asked.

"My opinion? He probably realized he was having a medical emergency. It would explain why he left the dining room in the first place. He probably started to feel some discomfort at that time. But like I said, it happened quick. There's nothing you could have done."

"You're sure about that?"

"Yes."

I wanted to hug Detective Medeiros. But of course I restrained myself.

"Thank you," I said.

"Okay." Medeiros said.

Medeiros and Donnie did that handshake-backslap-hug thing that guys do, and then Medeiros gave *me* a hug.

"I gotta get going," he said. "You have a nice evening. Nah, nah, I'll see myself out."

"So how'd our baby do at the doctor's?" Donnie asked when Medeiros had gone.

"She had a tough afternoon," I pulled up the chair that Medeiros had just been sitting in. It was still warm. "Francesca likes getting shots about as much as I do. It was kind of heartbreaking to watch her, actually."

"What are you doing?" Donnie asked. "Is something wrong?"

"Sorry, I'm still feeling a little queasy after what Detective Medeiros told us. I'm going to keep my head between my knees and try not to think about exploding blood vessels."

The baby squawked over the monitor.

"It's okay," Donnie said. "You stay there. I'll go get Francesca."

After a few minutes I was able to sit up like a normal person.

"So, this is great news, right?" I said. "I mean, not great that Stephen died, of course that's tragic, but at least you're not a murder suspect now. Right?"

"That's right."

"And we can get the bail money back now?"

"M-hm. It'll take a few weeks but yes."

"Did Medeiros say anything about how something like that can happen to someone so young?" I asked.

"He said there are factors that can increase your risk. Smoking. Certain recreational drugs. Steroids."

"Well, I guess that's... steroids? Really?"

"M hm. He said a lot of the high school boys are doing it now."

"And they can tell?"

"Ka`imi said the toxicology report's going to take a little longer. They'll know more when it's done."

Francesca was dozing in Donnie's lap, her fat cheek resting on his forearm. I reached over and stroked her fuzzy head.

"This is such a relief," I said. "I'm so glad—"

"Your name was the last word Stephen Park ever spoke," Donnie said. "I didn't think about it until today."

"It was the last thing *I* heard. But maybe he said other stuff afterwards. Like when he fell over the railing he said some swear words or something. Would that make you feel better?"

Donnie frowned.

"No, of course not."

"I feel bad for his parents."

Donnie touched Francesca's cheek. "Yeah. I do too."

"I wonder what they're going to do now."

"Probably just go back home," Donnie said. "What else is there?"

Chapter Forty-Five

THE NEXT MORNING, I was in the middle of filling out Student Retention Office forms when my phone rang. I saved my work and went to answer it. The caller ID was flashing Tiffany Schwartz's number.

I wasn't thrilled about having to talk to Stephen's mother, but at least it was a break from filling out Rodge Cowper's overdue paperwork.

Rodge hadn't filled out a single form all year, which meant I had to go back and do every single one for him in order to keep the department in compliance.

I reminded myself not to take it personally. This was the same Rodge who missed most of our department meetings and always turned in his grades late. Which mystified me, as he never gave out anything lower than an A, so what was the holdup? Rodge assigned no homework, he used class time to show videos or have "chat sessions," and his final exam was a beer party at his house. The only thing Rodge put any effort into was writing his own online reviews.

Because of his "student success" rates and stellar student evaluations, the Student Retention Office—the same Student Retention Office whose paperwork Rodge neglected—had once again anointed him Teacher of the Year. An honor that I had never once received.

But I wasn't bitter about it. Really.

"Molly, did you hear the news about Stephen? This is Tiffany by the way."

I brought the phone into the kitchen and poured myself a cup of coffee.

"I did hear about it. Detective Medeiros came to see us yesterday. Tiffany, I'm so sorry. If there's anything I can—"

"I just want to know who gave my

Stephen steroids," she interrupted. "Was it that P.E. teacher friend of his?"

"You mean Bee Corcoran? Gosh, I don't know. I mean, poor Bee is gone too now, of course. And as far as I know, the toxicology report hasn't come back yet. I guess we'll know more when it does."

I was pretty sure Bee Corcoran had been Stephen's source. She'd been using steroids in her rat studies, so she knew where to get them and how to use them. But I didn't want to fan the flames by saying any of this to Stephen's mother. And I could always be wrong.

"Well we're not just going to go away quietly," Stephen's mother insisted. "We need to find out what happened to our son. Everyone seems to be stonewalling us."

"Maybe Honey Akiona can help," I said.

"Who?"

"She was Donnie's lawyer—"

"We already have a lawyer."

"But Honey is tied in to the community. She went to school here and she has some good contacts. If you want to get to the bottom of this, I really think she's the one you want to talk to."

Stephen's parents got in touch with Honey Akiona. It turned out to be a good suggestion on my part, if I do say so myself. Honey contacted her old classmate Margaret Adams, who had recently relocated to Oregon. At Honey's request, Margaret persuaded Keola Shiner, who up until recently had worked for Bee Corcoran, to sit for an interview.

Keola didn't want to do the interview at first. But Margaret persisted, and finally, Keola agreed. He confirmed that he had worked in Bee's lab, and that he and Bee Corcoran had clashed because Bee kept "losing track" of the rats. She thought no one could tell the rats apart, he said, but he could. He'd had pet rats since he was a boy.

In the meantime, the toxicology reports came back on both Bee and Stephen. Both had traces of the identical combination of synthetic anabolic androgenic steroids. Which meant the whole time Bee had been preaching to me about the wonders of green tea and steamed broccoli and long walks, she'd been perfecting her own physique with illegal drugs. So Bee had been a bit of a phony too. Maybe she and Stephen deserved each other.

And then, as Honey Akiona was investigating for Stephen's parents, she dug up something else: Bee had been supplying Mahina State's football team with performance-enhancing drugs. (This was the biggest surprise so far. Our football team had an unbroken losing streak this season. How much worse would they have been without performance-enhancing drugs?)

Armed with this information, Stephen's parents made another run at the university. And this time, they were successful.

To make Stephen's parents go away (and quash any bad publicity about the football program), the university offered Stephen's parents a settlement. To Stephen's parents, it was insultingly small. When I heard the amount, though, I knew it was big enough to hurt Mahina State.

If we really had to fork over that much money to Stephen's parents, I knew we'd be buying our own toner and copy paper for the foreseeable future. Not that Stephen's parents didn't deserve some recompense, but still.

Stephen's parents decided they'd gotten the best deal they could, and prepared to return to California. Before they left, though, they wanted to say goodbye. Which is how Donnie and I ended up having lunch with them at the Lehua Inn Coffee Shop. (Their lawyer had already gone back to Los Angeles.)

We could hardly refuse their invitation, but I wasn't looking forward to it. Our good news, that Stephen had died of natural causes, was their bad news. While Donnie and I would be able to move on with our lives, Stephen's parents would be leaving Mahina bereaved and, in their view at least, practically empty-handed.

One thing I've always appreciated about Stephen's parents is that I never had to worry about awkward silences. As we waited for someone to come by and take our order, Stephen's mother went on (and on) about what a great influence I had been on Stephen. She told Donnie what a lifesaver I had been that time I bought Stephen a ticket and loaded him onto a plane, so his sister could meet him at LAX and take him straight to rehab.

"Did ye ken any o' this, Donnie?" Stephen's father asked.

"No," Donnie said truthfully. It had all happened before Donnie and I were dating, so I'd never seen any reason to tell him about it.

"What I don't understand is the steroid thing," Tiffany turned to me. "Are they sure about that?"

"I think so?" I stammered. Why was she asking me? I didn't do the autopsy. "I mean, that's what the medical examiner found."

"But what do you think?"

I shook my head. "I'm not a real doctor. As my mother often reminds me. But I do trust Honey Akiona. I know, it's hard to believe our football team has any kind of unfair advantage. I can't remember the last time they won a game."

"If you had stayed with Stephen this wouldn't have happened, Molly."

Poor Donnie. I reached under the table, found Donnie's hand, and squeezed it. He squeezed back.

"So many young men are using performance-enhancing drugs these days," I said. "Even in our high schools." That added nothing to the conversation, but I felt like I had to say some words.

"We'll be leaving wi' nothing," Stephen's father muttered.

"Less than nothing," Stephen's mother corrected him, "when you count what we paid for the lawyer. It's not like we need the money, Molly, but after how careless they were, your university should pay *something*. I mean, more than the pittance they're giving us. Don't you think? Angus, what about all of those safety things we have to do just to stay in business. Why should Mahina State get off without any penalty?"

"Our lawyer says if we tried to take it to court they'd drag it on for years." Stephen's father shook his head. "Like Tiff says, they're getting away wi' murder. It's no' right."

"Molly," Tiffany implored, "Tell me

something. First your university tried to convince us our son had been murdered, just to get themselves off the hook. Now they've talked our lawyer into settling for crumbs. Do they not have a conscience?"

"Well, since you asked," I said. "The problem is we can't afford to have a conscience. We genuinely don't have enough money to fix up our university and make it comply with all the laws we have to comply with. I used to hear people talk about it, but I never really believed it until I became department chair and saw the budget for myself."

"Well I know lawyers cost money," Tiffany countered. "Mahina State sure seems to have lawyers out the ying-yang."

"They're the university system lawyers. They're already paid for. The reason our university drags things out like this is number one, as I said, we don't have money, and number two, any bad publicity is going to scare off donors and students, and give the legislators a chance to flex their muscles on behalf of angry taxpayers by cutting our budgets even more."

"They shouldn't be able to get away with it, Molly." Tiffany's eyes were shining and rimmed with red now, although the rest of her face remained smooth and expressionless.

"Aye, they all expect us tae forget about our dead son and walk away," Angus agreed.

"Can't you think of something, Molly? You always were so clever."

Then, to my astonishment, Donnie said, "I have an idea."

Chapter Forty-Six

"THINGS SHOULD BE FEELING NORMAL AGAIN," I complained to Emma. "Stephen's death wasn't the university's fault, so the administration doesn't have to frame my husband for murder after all. We're going to get our bail money back soon, and life will go on. Why don't I feel relieved?"

"Because now you know our administration's so crooked they'd ruin your life to save themselves some money? And you know the prosecutor's in their pocket?"

"Yeah, those things are pretty disturbing. The other thing is that there were times when I thought Donnie really might have done it. I wish I didn't know that about myself. That I was capable of suspecting my own husband."

Through the window of my new office, I could see the old hospital building. I made a mental note to look for semi-sheer curtains. Something that would let the light in, but obscure the view of the building where Bee and Stephen had both lost their lives.

"Funny that both of 'em died the same way, yeah? In the same building," Emma grunted as she ripped the packing tape from a box. She seemed to intuit what I was thinking. "Almost like they both—"

"No, no, no, no."

"No what?"

I pulled out a disinfectant wipe and squatted to wipe down the dusty baseboards.

"Emma, I'm relying on you to reassure me. With your no-nonsense, science-based, anti-superstition point of view. Your job is to convince me that it's mere coincidence that two people died in a way that looks like the last thing they saw…"

"Was a ghost?"

I sighed.

"Yes."

"Yeah, I was kinda thinking the same thing, actually," Emma mused as she shelved my books in random order.

"What? Emma, you don't believe in ghosts. Besides, Stephen died of an aneurysm."

Emma wiped her hands on the back of her jeans and then ripped open another box.

"I don't believe in ghosts. But just cause I don't believe in 'em doesn't mean they don't exist."

"How is that helpful, Emma? Hint: it's not. Not when I'm moving in to this creepy old office."

"What's your problem, Molly? Scared of being in here by yourself?"

"No. Maybe."

"I can buy Park dying of natural causes," Emma went on. "He's been abusing his body for years, ah? With the smoking an' everything. But what made Bee bust through a fourth-floor railing? It's like she was running from something, scared for her life. An' they never figured out why, yeah?"

"Let's talk about something else," I said.

"Okay. Hey Molly, you wanna put anything in your secret room?"

"I don't know. I should at least air it out first. It's pretty musty in there." I felt the paneling for the soft spot, found it, and pushed. Nothing happened. Emma came up and gave it a shove, which did the trick. The door swung open.

The little room looked smaller than last time, probably because it had grown in my imagination.

"You gonna ask Facilities to put in a light?" Emma asked.

"No. I'm not going to tell Facilities about this space. They'll just take it away from me."

"Yeah, you're probably right. And they'll confiscate your door wedge while they're at it."

I went over to the window—which had much the same view as the other one—and unlatched it. I was able to muscle it open this time, although my efforts were rewarded with a shower of paint flakes.

"Eh, don't breathe that in, Molly," Emma warned. "It's probably full of lead."

"Shoot. Now I have to sweep it up."

"Ready to take a break?" Emma asked. "Let's fire up your coffee maker."

"Good idea. Remember how we used to sit around in my office with Pat and drink endless cups of coffee?

"Yeah. That was the good old days. Before you turned into a dorky suburban mom. Wanna call him?"

"Yeah, why not? All he can say is no."

It turned out Pat was at the downtown library doing research, and ready to take a break himself. He was at my office within five minutes. The coffee machine worked just fine and hadn't caused any fuses to blow or anything. The office smelled warm and homey.

"Whoa, did they finally buy you new chairs?" Pat exclaimed. Emma was already seated in one of my two matching mesh chairs, drinking her coffee.

"No, there's still no budget for office furniture. I had to pay out of pocket. My way of celebrating my new office. You want a coffee?"

"Sure. Wow, I get an actual chair!" He made a show of sitting down carefully, as if he had never seen an office chair before and wasn't sure what it was going to do.

"Molly's still sitting on her yoga ball, though," Emma said.

"I'm used to the yoga ball. A real office chair would feel weird now." I sat down on it with a bounce and brewed Pat a coffee. "These mugs are clean, by the way. Emma ran them through her autoclave. She says it's better than a dishwasher."

"You're welcome," Emma said.

Pat snorted as he took his cup. "What, like I care about germs? Coffee smells great, though. Thanks. Where's the baby?"

"Donnie has her."

"He brought her to the Drive-Inn?" Pat asked.

"Yeah, he wears the baby in that carrier thing," Emma said. "The girls think it's totally hot."

"They do?" I asked. "Which girls?"

"The girls that work there."

"What?"

"The customers, too. Come on, Molly, haven't you noticed? I mean, Donnie's already good looking. Strap a baby on him, and you can hear all the ladies ovulating when he walks by. Sounds like pennies dropping on a cookie sheet."

Pat shook his head and took a sip of coffee.

"Don't look at me. I'm not in this conversation."

"Let's talk about something else," I said. "Pat, are you still friends with that antique dealer? The one with the store down on the Bayfront?"

"He moved back to the mainland. Why?"

"Why is everyone moving back to the mainland? So inconsiderate of them. I wanted to see whether he could tell me what this thing was for. I found it here."

I dug the little engraved trowel out of my bag and handed it to Pat. He held it up to the window, looked at it from several angles, and set it on my desk.

"I'm stumped," he said. "Why don't you go online and do an image search?"

"We already did," Emma said. "The internet thinks it's a ski."

Pat set his coffee down on my desk and took out his phone.

"I still have his number. I'll text him a picture."

"Pat, you should take some more pictures while you're here," Emma said. "For your haunted Mahina articles."

"*Mysterious* Mahina," Pat corrected her.

"Whatever. It just stopped raining so the light's really good."

"I have more than enough pictures of this place," Pat said. "I just need to finish the installment I'm working on right now. That's what I was doing in the library."

"Didn't you say something about planting a camera somewhere?" I asked.

"Yeah, the ghost cam. It was a bust."

"Can't you just add some mysterious glowing lights or something to your video?" Emma asked. "What do the movie people say? Fix it in post."

"I'm not gonna add special effects. Give me some credit, Emma. I do have a few shreds of integrity left."

"Where were you filming?" I asked.

"The front entrance of the hospital building," Pat said. "I picked what I thought was the best angle. And before you ask, yes, I gave the police a copy of the video. Unfortunately, it wasn't any help. It didn't capture the place where Bee Corcoran died."

"But if you got the front of the building, they'd be able to see who went in and out," I said.

"The problem is a lot of people went in and out," Pat said. "And as you well know, Molly, the front door isn't the only entrance."

After a little prodding from Emma and me, Pat agreed to show us the video on his phone. I put on my reading glasses and watched as the building lit up with the sunrise. Over the next minute the light on the downhill side of the building grew brighter. First a trickle and then a flood of people flowed up the stairs, with only one or two going back down. Because the action was speeded up, the tree branches twitched comically and the people swarmed like cockroaches.

"Wait a minute," I said. "Can you slow this down?"

Pat took the phone back.

"See something the police missed, did you?"

"Maybe I did, Mr. Know-it-all."

I watched the video again, finger hovering over the pause symbol. When I saw what I was looking for I paused the playback.

"Here," I held the phone so Emma could see it. "Do you recognize her?"

"The smudge with the black hair?" Emma asked.

I took the phone back and zoomed in.

"No. Her."

"Oh. The smudge with the light brown hair," Pat said.

"And the blue shirt," I added. "Don't either of you see what I'm seeing?"

"How can you tell who it is?" Emma asked. "I can't even tell if it's a boy or a girl. Most of their face is behind that other lady with the long hair."

"Okay, but now. Look."

I took the phone back, started the video up, and paused it again.

"There. That's her leaving."

"Who?" Pat asked.

"Pat, it's Margaret!"

"Oh, Margaret." Emma leaned in for a closer look. "Yeah, it looks like her."

"Who's Margaret?" Pat asked.

"Margaret Adams. She took Intro to Business Management from me years ago. She was in the same class as Honey Akiona. She was working down at the bed and breakfast back then. That's not important. But she's been coming to my house every day and watching the baby."

"Oh yeah. That Margaret. The accounting major?"

"Really?" I said. "Accounting major is the one thing you remember about her?"

He squinted at the screen.

"Can you think of a better way to describe her in two words? Yeah, I guess it could be her."

"It is her," I said. "I remember she was

wearing a light blue shirt, because that's the same color I was wearing that day."

"I remember the blue shirt," Emma said. "Yours, Molly, not hers. Cause the milk stains, ah?"

"Pat," I asked. "what was the time of death? Bee's death?"

"How would I know?" Pat protested. "They haven't released any official—"

"We know you know," Emma interrupted him. "Just tell us."

Pat sighed.

"Fine. But don't tell anyone I told you."

"Yeah, yeah, Ida B. Wells," Emma said. "We know. You gotta protect your sources."

"Time of death was estimated between 6:30 and 10:30am," Pat said.

"So it could have been Margaret," I said. "If this really is her in the video. She could have killed Bee and then come over…"

"To watch your baby," Pat finished the thought for me.

"I don't like the way you put that," I said.

"So are you gonna tell Detective Medeiros about this?" Emma asked me.

"I don't know," I said. "I feel like I should ask Margaret about it first."

"Seriously?" Emma demanded. "Tell the murderer you figured out she's a murderer and then ask her if she thinks you should tell anyone else?"

"But Emma, it's Margaret Adams. She's not a murderer. She's an *accounting* major for crying out loud."

Pat's phone made a "plink" noise, and he swiped to see the message.

"Got it," he said. "Mystery solved."

"The murder?" Emma asked.

"No. Not the murder. The mystery of what your little ski is for. It's an absinthe spoon."

"Oh!" I picked it up and took another look.

"A what spoon?" Emma asked.

"Absinthe is a liqueur distilled from wormwood and flavored with herbs," I said. "You put a lump of sugar on the spoon and pour the liquid through."

"Why not just mix in the sugar the regular way?" Emma asked.

"I don't know. Tradition."

"Oh, Molly, I almost forgot," Pat said. "I found something out about your office. I think you'll be interested."

"Haunted?" Emma asked eagerly.

"Kind of. I was looking through some of the old local papers, and there's a pretty good chance that this was Constance Brigham's office."

"Constance Brigham. *The* Brighams? Son of a missionary marries the daughter of a chief, family amasses incredible wealth and influence? The ones with the house on Russian Road?"

"Yup, that's the family," Pat said.

"And whose office did you say this was?"

"Constance Brigham. She was the supervisor of the Inebriates Asylum. The whole thing was her project."

"Really? I got the boss's office?"

"Yeah, she was pretty unconventional," Pat said. "She didn't have to work at all, much less devote herself to running a rehab facility. She was supposed to get married off and become a society lady. But she drove off all her suitors and dedicated her life to this."

"Why have I never heard of her?" I asked.

"Because no one's written her biography," Pat said.

"Maybe you should do it," Emma suggested.

"I was actually thinking of doing a series on her," Pat said. "For *Island Confidential*. There's a pretty credible story about her early career, where she caught one of the doctors, old married guy, being inappropriate with a young patient. She confronted him about it, and the next day he was found dead on the hospital grounds. He'd thrown himself from the top floor. Or *someone* threw him."

"Wow." I said. "I can't say I feel too sorry for the guy, though. Is that callous of me, do you think?"

"Wait. Constance?" Emma asked. "Like Miss Constance? The avenging Miss Constance?"

"Maybe Constance was a common name back then," I said.

"Oh yeah, that's kind of a funny story," Pat said. "The legend of Miss Constance. I looked into it."

"And?" Emma and I asked in unison.

"It's from a book of Hawaiian ghost stories that was published in the early seventies. There's no written record of the legend before then that I can find. It seems like the author took the one incident from Constance Brigham's life and ran with it."

"Nah!" Emma objected. "Cannot be. The nineteen seventies?"

"That's right," Pat said.

"But me and all my friends—"

"Did you ever hear your parents ever talk about Miss Constance?" I asked.

"No, but…aw, man."

"There was a real Constance," Pat said. "But she wasn't a patient here, she ran the place. And she never had a husband."

"If Constance Brigham devoted her life to running the Inebriates Asylum," I said, "I'd have to assume she was a temperance advocate, right? How do you explain the absinthe paraphernalia?"

Pat picked up the spoon and examined it.

"Maybe she confiscated it from a patient," he said.

"Nah. I bet she was drinking it in her

secret office," Emma said. "And now you can continue the noble tradition, Molly. Don't worry, I'll help you. So you don't have to drink alone. It'll help you get your mind off thinking about Bee Corcoran anyway. I don't have to remind you how dangerous it is to go poking around unsolved murders."

"Please don't bring up the lava tube episode," I said. "But you're right, I should stop obsessing about it. Bee's death was ruled a suicide, Margaret is on the mainland, and most importantly, Donnie's off the hook. I'm through with murder investigations."

"That's more like it," Emma said.

Chapter Forty-Seven

AS SOON AS PAT LEFT, Emma asked,

"You think Constance Brigham and Miss Constance are the same person? Like Pat said?"

"Probably," I said. "Pat's good at researching that stuff. I hope he does write up something about her life. I'd read it."

"I like the avenging ghost version better."

"Well, someone already wrote *that* book. In the seventies."

"So speaking of innocent-seeming young women who go around slaughtering people," Emma said, "you gonna call Margaret or what?"

"Call Margaret? Weren't you just telling me how dangerous it would be—"

"Aw, come on, Molly. I was just saying that cause Pat was here and he's such a worry wart. Besides, I know you want to call her and ask her how come she's on Pat's surveillance tape."

"What makes you so sure about that?"

"Am I wrong?"

"I just can't reconcile it in my mind. Margaret was so conscientious. That's why we were comfortable having her watch the baby."

"And now you're dying to talk to her because you have to reassure yourself that you didn't leave your baby with a crazy murderer. Plus she's thousands of miles away so she can't hurt you."

Rather than continue to argue with Emma, I called Margaret's cell number. I had no clear plan of what I would say to her.

She sounded glad to hear from me.

"How's Francesca?" she asked. "Oh, I miss her so much! How's that little bottom tooth?"

"Extremely sharp, thanks for asking. Margaret, listen. I'm really sorry to bother you with this. But your boyfriend, Keola—"

"Husband," she said.

"Whoa, what? You got married?"

I felt a little stung that I hadn't been invited to the wedding, forgetting for a moment that I suspected Margaret of murder.

"We kind of eloped," she said.

"Did Honey Akiona know that? She called you, right, and talked to Keola about Bee's rat experiment and why he left her lab?"

"Oh yes, Honey knows."

"Wow. Congratulations. I guess everyone knows but me. Anyway, here's why I called. Did you know about Bee Corcoran passing away? She was found dead the day you left the island."

"I…yes."

I looked at Emma for some kind of nonverbal moral support, but she was playing a game on her phone.

"Margaret, the police have video of you

going into the hospital building the morning of Bee Corcoran's death."

It was true. The police did have the tape, even if they didn't know who was on it.

Margaret made a little squeak.

"And you're on the video leaving a few minutes later. You're wearing the same cornflower blue top you were wearing when you showed up to my house to watch Francesca that day."

Margaret was quiet.

"Margaret, is someone there with you?"

"No. No, he's at work."

"Margaret," I persisted, "Did you kill Bee Corcoran, and then come over to my house and spend the day with my daughter? I'm not taping this conversation or anything, I just have to know."

"No, Professor, it wasn't like that. I would never hurt Dr. Corcoran. Or Francesca, if that's what you're thinking. I would never hurt anyone!"

But she wasn't denying having been at the hospital building when Bee died.

I remembered a phrase that I'd heard from an executive coach. When you want to grab someone by the shoulders and shake them, say this instead: *Help me understand.*

"Margaret, help me understand. What happened?"

"Professor, I don't know what happened. I mean, I do know, but I don't…"

"Can you tell me what you remember? Please?"

Emma looked up from her phone, interested.

"Did you go to Bee's lab?" I asked. "Dr. Corcoran's lab?"

"Yes. Professor, we only left Mahina because Keola couldn't find another job that paid as well as being Dr. Corcoran's lab assistant. If she'd hired him back, we could have stayed. So it was our last day, and I just wanted to talk to her myself. That's all. I just went to talk to her."

"So what happened?" I asked.

"The door was open so I let myself in. Dr. Corcoran was standing over by the window, you know, at the end of that long counter? She looked like she was writing something in a book. I guess I was pretty quiet, so she didn't notice me come in."

Emma was now leaning into my phone and listening, wide-eyed.

"I walked over to her, but she didn't look up, and I didn't want to interrupt her. So I waited until she was finished writing and she closed the notebook and put it away, and then she looked up and saw me, and before I could even say anything…"

Margaret took some time to compose herself before she continued. "I guess I startled her. It was like, she kind of screamed a little bit when she saw me? And then she stumbled and went backwards out the window. It was open, I think to let some air in, because it was kind of hot and stuffy. Anyway, it was so fast. One minute she was there, and then next thing I knew she was gone…I started to go out after her but I saw the railing was broken and I knew it wasn't safe to go out on the balcony. I'd left my phone in the car because I'd been charging it. I tried to call for help from the landline but it didn't work."

"You *tried* to call for help? *Did* you call for help?"

"The phone was dead. There was no dial

tone. Then I saw a cardboard box sitting in front of the window, which I think was what she'd tripped over. I hope this wasn't wrong of me, Professor, but I saw Keola's lab coat sitting on top of it. I realized it was Keola's box. He'd been packing his things to leave, and he'd left his stuff there where he thought it would be out of the way, but it wasn't really, he'd left it in the worst possible place, because Dr. Corcoran...I moved the box away from the window. I hope Keola's not in trouble because of me."

"Does Keola know any of this?" I asked.

"No," she sniffled. "He doesn't know I went in that morning. I don't think he even knows about Dr. Corcoran being dead. We've both been so busy, you know I haven't told anyone about—"

"What did you do then?" I asked. "After you realized the lab phone wasn't hooked up?"

"I ran to the one open door on the hallway. It was the department office. The only person in there was a student worker. I told her to call nine one one, that Dr. Corcoran was hurt."

"Did she?"

"She looked around kind of confused, like someone had to give her permission, so I told her, hurry, and she said okay, and started looking around the desk for the phone. I left but I assumed she made the call."

"Why didn't you stay and wait for someone to show up, so you could explain what happened?" I asked. "It would have saved a lot of people a lot of grief."

"I'm so sorry," she said quietly. "If I could go back and do it over...I guess I wasn't thinking. All I was thinking was I couldn't be late."

"Late for what?"

"To watch Francesca."

"You'd just watched someone fall out a fourth-floor window and you were worried about being *late*? Margaret, I would have understood. Really."

"What's that sound?"

"Coffee machine." I glared at Emma, who was noisily brewing herself another cup.

She gave me a "what am I supposed to do?" shrug.

"Professor, what's going to happen now? I understand if you have to report us."

Margaret's story added up (if you will). I had found a notebook in the drawer at the end of that long counter. Now that I knew its contents, I understood why Bee wanted to keep it hidden. We had found the lab phone off the hook, which was consistent with Margaret having tried to make a call. It hadn't been hooked up, so she didn't get a dial tone. Margaret said she'd moved Keola's box away from the window, which was why the young man had asked us whether we'd moved his stuff.

It seemed clear to me that Bee's death had been an accident. Margaret couldn't have staged it if she'd tried. No one knew how fragile the railing was. Neither Margaret nor Keola (and probably not even both of them together) seemed capable of overpowering the athletic Bee and pushing her to her death.

And thanks to my own experience with student workers, I knew it was entirely plausible that the ball had been dropped on

FRANKIE BOW

the 9-1-1 call, leaving the security guard to discover Bee's body.

"I don't think it's my place to report anything," I said. "If you want to pursue it, I think you should get legal advice. I recommend Honey Akiona. But they've already put it down to suicide. So maybe it's best to just let things be."

"Oh, thank you so much, professor."

"Okay, well, thank you for letting me know what happened. It's—"

"Professor? Wait, don't hang up. There was something I wanted to talk to you about. I was thinking about calling you, in fact. And now that you called me, I think it's kind of like a sign."

"Really? Okay. What is it?"

"It's about the Arts and Sciences dean. Geoffrey Gunderson."

Chapter Forty-Eight

IT TURNED out Margaret's new husband Keola had been sitting on a lot more information than we knew.

Bee Corcoran's lab was supposed to have been upgraded to Biosafety Level 2, but the money for the improvements hadn't come through. Geoffrey Gunderson, it turns out, had been skimming money from the NIH grant that had been funding Bee Corcoran's lab.

Most of the funds had been diverted to Ray Pang's re-election fund. So Pang, in misdirecting Stephen's parents' lawsuit, wasn't just trying to bank a future favor with the university. He had been doing the bidding of a major campaign donor.

Gunderson wasn't the hapless messenger boy of some higher up; the plan, it seemed, was entirely his. The lawsuit from Stephen's parents, focusing on code violations in the old hospital building, would have brought unwelcome scrutiny, and risked exposing Gunderson's illegal activities.

Gunderson was not in cahoots with Bee Corcoran. She didn't know he'd been diverting money from her existing NIH grant, nor that he was planning to do the same with her system research award. Dean Gunderson, in turn, had no idea Dr. Corcoran was fudging her research results. He'd picked her research for the system life sciences award simply because he thought it had a good chance of winning. And he was right.

An investigation confirmed Keola's claims. Mahina State University had to pay back Bee's grant. Keola and Margaret got a whistleblower payout of thirty percent of the total, which was a big help to the young couple. As for Geoffrey Gunderson, he incurred the usual penalty meted out to administrators in such situations: A large severance payout and a quiet move to a higher-paying job at another institution.

I'm not sorry I squirted him with breast milk.

Chapter Forty-Nine

I'D HAD ENOUGH of university events, but we couldn't really get out of attending the blessing ceremony for the official opening of the old Mahina Memorial Hospital building. Donnie, Francesca, and I found an empty table near the back of the dining hall. The place looked less glamorous in the daytime than it had at the donor dinner. The sun shone through the tall windows, highlighting every mismatched paint patch and missing ceiling tile. I texted Pat and Emma to let them know where we were, then took the seat closest to the wall and popped the baby under my top. Donnie went to get me a glass of water.

"Molly!" I heard a familiar voice behind me. It took me a moment to place it. I turned around to see Stephen Park's mother, Tiffany Schwartz. She wore a floor-length gown encrusted in flashing red sequins. It was a little dressy for Mahina, especially for an afternoon event.

"Tiffany! Hi! Sorry, I can't get up right now."

Francesca was vacuuming milk out of me with a vengeance. And I was so thirsty it was painful. Where was Donnie with that water?

"Oh, did you hurt yourself?" Tiffany asked.

"No, I just..." I glanced down at Francesca's little pink toes, curling and uncurling.

"Never mind," she said, "there's Angus. Angus! Over here, sweetheart!"

Stephen's father strode over, looking both stylish and sweaty. A blazer over a turtleneck was not what I would have picked for un-air-conditioned building on a summer afternoon in Mahina. Most of the men in the room were wearing cotton aloha shirts.

"Oh, you're both here," I said. "How wonderful. Would you like to join us?"

"No, we're sitting up at the front table," Tiffany said. "We'd better get up there. Where's Donnie?"

"Right here." Donnie set two glasses of water in front of me. I picked up one and downed it gratefully, then started on the other one. Donnie hugged Tiffany and shook Angus's hand. Then Tiffany said,

"Did you tell her?"

"No," Donnie said. "I thought she'd get a kick out of being surprised."

When Stephen's parents had left, I said,

"Where did you get the idea I like surprises?"

"I didn't say you'd *like* it," he said, picking up the two empty cups. "I said you'd get a *kick* out of it. I'll be back with more water."

Pat and Emma showed up and took their seats at our table. Donnie came back just as Victor Santiago, Mahina State University's Vice-President for Student Outreach and

Community Relations, stepped up to the microphone.

We sat through Santiago's brief history of the building. He talked up the architectural features and left out the part about it having been a tuberculosis hospital. Then came a series of speeches from various administrators I knew only by sight. Finally, the chancellor stepped up and said a few appreciative words about our donors.

Emma leaned over and whispered,

"What are they gonna name the building? I missed it."

"They haven't said," I told her.

Donnie smiled, but didn't say anything.

An eruption of applause yanked my attention back up to the front. Victor Santiago was at the mic again, and Angus Park and Tiffany Schwartz were walking up to where he was standing.

"Why are Stephen's parents up there?" I whispered to Donnie. "They didn't donate money, did they? Weren't they just suing us?"

"The university agreed to give them naming rights to the building," Donnie said.

"What? Instead of money?"

"Exactly."

I stared at him.

"That's what you were suggesting at lunch that day?"

Donnie nodded.

"Donnie, you're amazing."

He settled his arm around my shoulders, and we watched our Vice-President for Student Outreach and Community Relations present Stephen's parents with a scale model of the building, complete with its new sign.

So Stephen's parents had gotten some compensation from the university after all, and I wouldn't have to pay out of pocket for my department's printer paper.

When the presentation was over, we all walked to the next building over to show Donnie my new office. He was mildly impressed by the extra room, but more interested in the secret doorway.

"This is solid." He ran his fingers down the door jamb and examined the recessed latch. "You don't find work like this anymore."

Emma and Pat were sitting in my visitor chairs. Emma was trying to goad Pat into a game of bumper cars by scooting her chair into him repeatedly.

"This is why we can't have children in the office," I said.

Donnie stood up, his hand still on the door jamb.

"Is Francesca okay?"

Pat placed one big boot on the base of Emma's chair, rolled her away from him, and held her at leg's length.

"I'm not talking about Francesca," I said.

"I was kinda surprised by the name they picked." Bored with bumper-chairs, Emma stood and went through the doorway into the secret room. "I thought they'd want to call it the Stephen Park Building or something."

Donnie frowned.

"I thought so too. But I suppose Park Beverly Hills Cosmetic Center Building was what they wanted. What are you going to use the extra room for, Molly?"

"I'm going to use it as a private place to pump milk," I said.

"It's a bar," Emma called out.

Donnie looked at me.

"I wouldn't call it a *bar*," I said. "I mean, it's not just a bar. I ran an extension cord in so I have a coffee machine and a mini fridge. But yes, people can come here after hours to relax if they like. Including and especially my hardworking husband."

"Get some A/C in here and you got yourself a deal," Donnie said.

"Really?"

"Donnie," Emma called out, "you want some absinthe?"

"The liqueur?" Donnie asked.

"Yeah. You want to try it?"

"Uh, no thank you. It's a little early. In fact, I should probably head back to work."

"Aw, brah, you leaving already?" Emma came out holding a silver tray. On it were three plain glasses that used to be furikake jars, a green Pernod bottle, a bowl of ice, a smaller bowl of sugar cubes, and the fancy spoon I'd found in the back of the drawer.

Donnie checked his watch. "Maybe some other time, Emma. The dinner crowd's going to be coming in pretty soon."

"Papa's gotta work to build up that college fund," I nuzzled the top of the baby's fuzzy head. "Right, Francesca?"

"College fund?" Donnie put on an innocent look. "Oh, I have bigger plans than that. I was thinking if I keep at it and play my cards right, maybe one day this will be the Donnie's Drive-Inn Building."

About the Author

Frankie Bow teaches at a public university and writes licensed Miss Fortune World novellas as well as The Professor Molly Mysteries. Unlike Professor Molly, Frankie is blessed with delightful students, sane colleagues, and a perfectly nice office chair.

Thank you for taking the time to read The Perfect Body. If you enjoyed it, please consider telling your friends and posting a short review. Word of mouth is an author's best friend and much appreciated.
    Mahalo, Frankie